THE UPRISING

THE MAPMAKERS IN CRUXCIA

EIRLYS HUNTER
ILLUSTRATIONS BY KIRSTEN SLADE

GECKO PRESS

For Idris and Laurence, with love

PRAISE FOR THE MAPMAKERS' RACE

Selected for the International Board on
Books for Young People (IBBY) Honour List 2020

Chosen for The Reading Agency UK Summer Reading Challenge

Chosen for Australian Indie Booksellers Summer Reading Guide

"The Mapmakers' Race already feels like a timeless adventure … a thrilling tale full of derring-do and heart." BOOK TRUST, UNITED KINGDOM

"One of the most poised, stylish children's books I've read in a long time."
KATE DE GOLDI, RADIO NEW ZEALAND

"I love this!" KIM HILL, RADIO NEW ZEALAND

"An adventure story of such quality and originality, pace and punch."
BOOKWAGON, UNITED KINGDOM

"This rip-roaring adventure about four kids and a parrot called Carrot is classic read-aloud fare." BEST KIDS BOOKS 2018, *NEW ZEALAND LISTENER*

"A thrilling adventure tale." *THE IRISH TIMES*

"I loved this tale of ingenuity, exploration and nature."
BETTER READ KIDS BOOKSTORE, AUSTRALIA

"Full of danger, excitement and adventure with wonderfully memorable characters, this is one not to be missed."
RICKARO BOOKSHOP, UNITED KINGDOM

"Will have some children reaching for ink and paper to become wondrous mapmakers, and others out in the wilderness, exploring and making tracks. Charming, exciting and just a little dangerous."
VOLUME BOOKSTORE, NEW ZEALAND

"A thrilling and thoroughly enjoyable adventure full of setbacks and dangers and family squabbling, but also fun and laughter and the thrill of exploration and storytelling around campfires under the open stars." *CHILDREN'S BOOKS IRELAND*

"This is good old-fashioned storytelling, a classic quest with challenges in every chapter, a well-thought-out narrative arc and plenty of in-jokes for all ages." *NEW ZEALAND BOOKS*

Contents

ONE	Beyond Porto Pearls	1
TWO	Cruxcia	10
THREE	Cowboys	22
FOUR	How Humphrey Saved the Day	29
FIVE	A Lot of "Whys?" and Some "Becauses"	43
SIX	Progress and Progress	52
SEVEN	Land Grabbing	57
EIGHT	Outrageous Desecration	60
NINE	The Chase	65
TEN	The Prison	76
ELEVEN	Spying	81
TWELVE	Amazement	89
THIRTEEN	The Wisps of a Plan—and Scrolls	93
FOURTEEN	A Genius Idea	99
FIFTEEN	Emp ire Hot el Odo	103
SIXTEEN	Maps and Plans	109
SEVENTEEN	A Secret, Risky Meeting	115
EIGHTEEN	The Road to Bereff Stonch	123
NINETEEN	Three Amazing Things	136
TWENTY	Going Up	141

TWENTY-ONE Never, Ever, Ever Again		145
TWENTY-TWO Which Way?		154
TWENTY-THREE Tired, Cold, Hungry and Sore		160
TWENTY-FOUR Kleffi and Tage		169
TWENTY-FIVE Cousins		175
TWENTY-SIX Paint and Pyrotechnics Workshop		180
TWENTY-SEVEN The Land Court		190
TWENTY-EIGHT Will This Change Everything?		202
TWENTY-NINE Lysander's Performance		212
THIRTY Meanwhile…		218
THIRTY-ONE The Sky Worff		236
THIRTY-TWO The Party		243

Chapter One

Beyond Porto Pearls

"Where are we? What is this place?" Sal stood, half-asleep, beside the coach that seemed to have stopped in the middle of nowhere.

"Quick, grab your things and hurry," said Ma. "Hang onto Humphrey, Sal."

The coachman passed the last bag down from the roof. Ma shouldered her rucksack, picked up the carpetbag and the tool bag and strode away towards some bright lights.

The night was starry black, and cold. They all heaved their rucksacks onto their shoulders and Francie followed Ma, with Carrot the parrot on her arm. Sal picked up the picnic basket and towed a sleepy Humphrey.

"Joe, come *on*." He'd stopped to stare at the sky. Sal yawned and shivered. "Hurry up!"

Joe came reluctantly. "So many stars."

There was a low building ahead. Light poured out of the door every time it opened. Inside, a queue of people with bags and boxes curled round a waiting-room and was exiting through another door on the far side. Ma told them to join it while she went to talk to a uniformed man. She returned clutching tickets. "We made it. Just in time."

The sign on the far door seemed to be written in several languages, but included the words LAWNCHARIUM, SKY WORFF and EMBARKKASHON TOWER. The letters GTC were printed below the sign.

"Embarking on what?" Sal whispered to Joe. "I'm not sure about this."

Francie hugged her stomach.

Ma had refused to tell them how they were getting to Cruxcia, saying it was a special surprise and they'd love it. The queue shuffled forward slowly, then before long they were outside. Ahead of Sal, people were climbing a flight of steps, lit by lanterns. Steps to what? Sal craned her neck to make out a vast whale shape, basking in the air high above them.

"Holeygamoley," she whispered.

Humphrey hid his face in her back. "What is it?"

"I think it's a dirigible," said Sal. "We're going on an airship!"

The dirigible was tethered to a tower. The queue stretched up the steps to the landing stage. This was too exciting, and very scary, though Ma seemed completely calm. She went first, up the stairs, across a gangway that bobbed and wobbled, and into the boat that hung under the giant balloon. It was like a cross between a ferry and a charabanc, with two rows of bench seats facing forward, three people to a seat, and a walkway down the middle. Twelve rows, seventy-two people, Sal counted automatically.

A woman wearing a flying suit looked at their tickets and pointed to the bench that spanned the back of the boat. So lucky! They'd be able to watch the world disappear behind them. But there was nothing to stop them or their things from falling overboard. Sal could already feel her worry warring with the thrill of viewing the world from above.

She squeezed Humphrey's arm and made him look at her. "No leaning over, not even a finger past the rail, understand? Or you'll be dead."

He nodded, eyes huge. "When will we see Pa? Today? Tomorrow?"

"If only," said Joe.

"Today we're going to Cruxcia because we found out that's where Pa's expedition went," said Sal. "Then we have to find out if they're still there, or if they went somewhere else. There are loads of different countries in Grania. But everyone has to be somewhere. We just have to find him."

"I'm good at looking," said Humphrey.

"You are. You're an excellent looker," said Sal.

They sat as still as they could in their seats, and watched four uncooperative sheep and crates of chickens being loaded into storage below their deck. The sky began to lighten in the east and gradually the night turned from black to grey.

Humphrey peered cautiously over the back. "Sal, Sal, there's giant birds!"

Three strange objects with outstretched wings were poised beside the landing strip. They *did* look like giant birds. They had letters painted on their tails. Sal squinted. GTC.

"Those must be ornithopters," said Ma. "They're for transport. One day we might go in one."

A man on the platform blew a whistle, the door in the boat's side was closed and bolted, and the gangway pulled back onto the landing stage.

Sal had been watching a smudge of dust move along the road from Porto Pearls. It was a four-horse carriage, driving at speed towards the Embarkkashon Tower.

As the tethering ropes fell away, the airship quivered and shuddered beneath her, and slowly began to rise.

Below, two figures, one tall, the other short, scrambled out of the carriage and ran to the steps.

Too late for them: the dirigible was on its way.

The balloon rose, with its ferry boat slung beneath it, and the silent land shrank away. Sal felt as if she were dreaming—even more when the airwoman pulled on ropes and huge maroon and cream striped sails unfurled below the boat. It was all so beautiful, her eyes prickled.

Ma called over the wind, "Someone hang on to Carrot in case she's tempted to fly. She'd never keep up."

But Carrot had more sense than that. She didn't even want to see where they were going. She walked down Joe's leg, muttering "Riduckulous, Ridonkulous". She played with his bootlace for a moment, then scuttled under the bench seat.

The sun rose behind the eastern hills, giving the whale and the boat a pair of shadows that chased along the ground together. Francie couldn't stop smiling. She got out her sketchbook and started to draw this upside-down world: the whale swimming through air, the boat hanging under the whale, and the sails stretching down towards the land.

Sal turned her attention to the balloon. She stared at the small pod above them, suspended from the middle of the whale, wondering if it contained a pilot. "I'd like to ask the airwoman how this works," she said to Joe. "She might be able to explain the relationship between the upward motion from the gas in the balloon and the forward thrust from the engine and sails. And how they steer."

"Save me!" said Joe.

The airwoman continued adjusting ropes and checking dials. Sal wasn't brave enough to interrupt her.

"Breakfast time," said Ma, and handed out cheese pastries from the picnic basket. "They're a specialty of Grania."

Crunchy, flaky, cheesy—delicious!

They passed over a toy village clustered around toy trees, and they waved to tiny toy figures who ran out and waved back. They rose over steep cliffs, cut through with ravines. Humphrey pointed out a long procession of camels crossing a red plain, but none of the riders took any notice of the dirigible, even when Humphrey shouted: "Hey, camels. Up here, camels!"

"You're a camel. A camel with no humps," said Joe.

"No, I'm not."

"Oh, yes you are. And you're Hump-free!"

It took him a moment to get it.

Sal pointed to GTC printed on the inside of the door. "What does that stand for, Ma? It was on the ornithopters, and in Porto Pearls too."

"The Granian Trading Company," said Ma. "I don't know much about it—it's quite secretive. They come from overseas to trade. They buy things in one place and take them somewhere else to sell. Before they started this dirigible service, the only way to get to Cruxcia was six days on a camel—I decided that six days is five and a half days too long for a camel ride."

"Good decision," said Sal. "This is the best thing ever."

It was good to do nothing but watch the world drift by below them, especially after yesterday, which they'd spent in the steamy, stinky, scary bustle of Porto Pearls. The captain of the boat that had taken them there said it should rightly be called Pirate City. Sal was glad they'd only had to stay two nights. They'd seen shocking things in the city: the row of rags that turned out to be a family sleeping in the street, or children and grown-ups begging (including a man with a wooden leg, like an actual pirate). Worst of all, everyone else in the town just stepped around the homeless, hungry families as if they were invisible.

One good thing about Porto Pearls was the map shop. Sal hadn't known there was such a thing. Thousands of maps hung from its walls, or were rolled up in cubby holes, piled on tables and stacked in racks. New maps, old maps, printed maps and hand-drawn maps. Ma needed a map of the region to start planning the search for Pa, and while she was deciding which one, Francie and Sal flicked through a rack. They were amazed to discover that some of the maps had been drawn by people they knew, or had heard of. They found a map of the Coralian Alps by Monty Basingstoke-Black and one of East Smoke Island by Agatha Amersham—they'd both been on the Great Mapmaking

Race which the Santanders had won. Their winnings were paying for this expedition to find Pa.

Then Francie spotted the name Waldo Watkins in the corner of a map—the friend Pa was working with when he never came home. And it was dated eight months ago! She showed it to Ma, who immediately bought that map too. And all the time, a tall woman and a short man had stood in a dark corner of the shop, whispering together and watching them. They made Sal feel very uncomfortable. Later, Joe and Francie had seen them again in the hotel.

The shop assistant told Ma that he'd bought Waldo Watkins's map from a nun from the infirmary, who'd sold it to pay for the care of a sick patient. So they set off for the infirmary.

"Could that patient be Pa?" asked Joe.

"No," said Ma, "I'm sure it's not Pa."

They'd crossed Porto Pearls in a cab, and all the way there Sal had thought, *please let it be Pa*. And then she thought, *but only if he's getting better*. She'd almost convinced herself that they'd find him sitting in a dressing gown in the infirmary garden recovering from a terrible illness.

It wasn't Pa. At the infirmary a nun explained to Ma that Waldo Watkins had been the patient. He'd been very sick and died of Desert Fever. The nun gave Ma a small bag containing all his possessions, which made Ma cry and squeeze Sal's hand too tight. They gave three gold coins to the infirmary to thank the nuns for looking after him.

On the way back to their hotel Humph was quiet, then he whispered, "Why did Wallo Watky die? Was he old?"

Ma put an arm round Humphrey. "Yes, he was old. Too old to still be working, really, but he loved making maps and he had no family to stay home for. He told Pa he'd taken this job, that the pay was good, and why not come with him? Pa's last letter to us came from here. It said they were going to meet someone called Zander Abercrombie for final details before setting off the next day, and we might not hear from him for some time, as they'd be far from any postal offices."

"This was just their starting point. They could have gone anywhere," said Sal.

"I'm afraid they could," said Ma.

"Do you think Pa is dead, too?" Humph asked in a mouse's voice.

"No," said Ma. "I believe he's alive, and I'm certain that we're going to find him."

She opened Waldo Watkins's bag of possessions. "Now what's in here?"

There was a pencil box, which Ma gave to Humphrey to encourage him to practise writing, and a drawing pad, which she flicked through. There were sketches of rock formations and studies of trees and leaves, but most of the pages were blank. She gave it to Francie.

Then she pulled out a cylindrical case. Ma smiled. "I feel certain that Waldo would have said, 'Give this to Joe.'"

Joe opened the lid of the leather case and tipped out a tube of dark wood with brass ends. He pulled one end and the tube grew—it was a telescope. He clutched it tight. It was the thing he wanted most in all the world.

The last thing in the bag was a coin purse. It was empty. "Here, Sal, you have this. Waldo was very fond of you when he met you as a baby. He'd be pleased to think that a nearly grown-up Sal was using something of his." Sal fingered the tooled red leather. The purse had compartments, and a clasp that shut with a satisfying snap. She was pleased that Ma realised she was growing up.

Chapter Two

CRUXCIA

"I'm cold," said Joe.

"For goodness' sake, put your hat and jacket back on," said Ma.

Joe put on all his extra layers. It was a relief having Ma to tell him what to do again. They hadn't had Ma on the Great Race, but they did have Beckett, a boy who was older than Sal and could find food anywhere—and cook it. He'd always believed that they would finish the Race with Beckett's help, but he'd never felt completely safe, as he did now Ma was back in charge.

The dirigible rose as the land rose and in mid-afternoon they sailed above a vast uncultivated plain rimmed with snow-patched mountains. Francie pointed out antelope grazing, a herd of wild horses and tracks leading across the plain between tiny settlements. Joe took out his new telescope and watched the animals galloping together. He saw that the settlements were clusters of big round tents.

Back in the hotel room after the infirmary visit yesterday, Joe had been fiddling with his pocket knife when Francie appeared with Wally Watkins's drawing pad under her arm and gestured at the window. Joe stood up. "Ma, can me and Francie explore the garden?"

"If you promise to stay in the hotel grounds."

Francie nodded approval at Joe. She never spoke, but he usually knew what she was thinking and feeling. Outside, they crossed the gravel path to a bench seat and she opened the sketchbook across their laps.

The drawing of a landscape covered both pages. There was a mountain range in the background, with a deep valley running

into it. In the middle of the valley was a hemispherical hill covered in trees, and nearby, a town of towering buildings on another hill. To one side was a market with stalls and animals, and sitting on a rock in the foreground, with a mug in his hand, was Pa. Positively, definitely Pa.

"Ma must have flicked straight past it," said Joe softly and Francie nodded. "So, now we need to find out where this is." They grinned at each other.

They showed the picture to the man at the reception desk, but he only shrugged and so did the woman polishing the stair rail. Two men crossed the lobby and entered a room on the far side. The sign on the door said SMOKING ROOM. Joe looked at Francie, who was trying to be braver about people. "Follow them?"

She nodded but he could feel her worry pulsing out. He gestured "ears" and she pulled back her hair to show that she'd already stuffed them with cotton wool. Loud noises terrified Francie.

The room was almost silent. Newspapers rustled softly as their pages were turned, and people spoke in murmurs. The loudest noise was the chink of ice in a glass, then a match was struck to keep a pipe alight. Pipe and cigar smoke hung in a pall above people's heads. The smoke stung Joe's eyes and smelt horrible. Several people glanced up at them with disapproval. Joe felt Francie tense up, but she followed close behind as he tiptoed across the thick carpet.

He spoke quietly to the men sitting around a table. "Excuse me, but would any of you know where this is?" He pointed at the book Francie held open.

One man said, "No idea, sorry," and the others shrugged and shook their heads.

The people in the high-backed sofas by the window didn't know either. When the group between the potted palms also shrugged, Francie held up a hand to Joe. She pulled a pencil from her hair and found an empty page. Her hand flew over the paper until she had made a copy of the map Ma had bought of the whole region. Francie had only looked at it for a couple of minutes, but she'd remembered the routes, the settlements, and even some of the names. Joe's twin was a brilliant artist.

She drew a careful question mark in the corner, then held up the picture, pointing and raising her eyebrows. Francie was an expert at communicating without words.

A woman in a feathery hat murmured to an elderly man with a long grey beard. He squinted his watery eyes at the map and the picture. Finally, he took Francie's pencil and with shaking fingers circled a town on her map. He gestured to the town in the picture. "Croosha," he said. "This is Croosha."

Joe took the pencil and wrote CROOSHA.

The man shook his head and wrote CRUXCIA.

"Cruxcia! Thank you," said Joe. "You did it, Francie!" He squeezed her hand, and said, "Thank you, thank you," again, and one or two people even smiled at them.

"Excuse me," said a slimy voice. It was the short man who had stared at them in the map shop. He was sitting at the bar with the tall woman. The tips of his moustache pointed to his ears. "May I look?"

Joe felt Francie sizzle with fear, which he didn't understand;

the man made him angry. "No," he said. "I'm afraid it's private," and they ran upstairs to tell Ma and the others that they'd found out where they needed to go next.

The dirigible began to descend as it approached the mountains. They were flying over mile after mile of brown bushes in rows, and beyond that was a green and beige valley with the tree-covered hill from the picture. And there was the town with towers: Cruxcia. They were in the right place.

The ground grew closer and they could see the market from the drawing, and a tethering tower. The airship's sails were furled, the engine was cut, ropes lowered and caught by someone on the platform, and the dirigible was winched down until the boat was alongside the landing stage. As they waited to disembark, they heard clanking, as a maroon and cream ornithopter flapped in low and rolled onto the landing strip just beyond the airship. Joe and Humph stared at the great mechanical bird, and Francie drew it in her sketchbook.

The door was unlatched and a gangway attached. Joe let Humph be first off and followed him down the steps. Nearby, the belly of the ornithopter was lowered and steps set up beneath it. Two people disembarked—one tall, one short. Even from a distance they were familiar.

Joe waited for the others to come down the steps, then he grabbed Ma's arm. "Those two! Tall and Short! They stared at us in the map shop. And they were in the hotel." He explained about the Smoking Room.

"I saw them, too," said Sal. "They got to the launch platform just after we cast off. They looked furious at missing the flight."

"It might be nothing to do with Pa, but they were interested in the map and the picture of Cruxcia, and now they're here, and I don't trust them, Ma."

"I don't like the sound of it either," said Ma. "Thank goodness you're all such noticing children. I'll try and find out who they are. Meanwhile, be like mongooses. Watch out for each other and know your nearest hidey-hole."

It was a long walk from the landing stage to the nearest city gate, but the air was cool and crisp—much better for walking than the sweaty heat of Porto Pearls.

A dirt road ran through the middle of the market and Ma stopped at a stall selling drinks. Joe, Francie and Sal each chose a fresh coconut with a wooden straw stuck through the husked shell. Ma and Humph had squeezed lemon drinks with mint and ice.

Humphrey looked around, peering at everyone.

"What are you doing?" asked Joe.

"Looking for Pa."

"Good for you." It could happen like that. Pa could just be sitting on the side of the road, with no money to get home. But Joe knew it probably wouldn't be that easy. They might not find him at all. Or they might find out that he'd died—no, he wasn't going to let that thought into his head.

The market stretched for miles. They stopped to admire a pen of baby goats and to stroke donkeys that tried to nibble their shirt sleeves. People rode past on horses with fancy saddles, then a string of camels ambled by. "Hoity-toity!" Carrot screeched from Joe's shoulder. A camel stretched out its very long neck and spat at Carrot—luckily it missed, because the spit smelled horrible.

There were stalls selling unfamiliar vegetables and fruits, and spices that made Francie sneeze. If you needed a saucepan, or a flute or a new shirt, this was the place to come, and if you were hungry, there were rows of stalls selling steaming bread and black stuff on sticks. Some of it didn't even look like food, but it smelled good.

They stopped to listen to a man singing; people were laughing and throwing coins into his hat. The chorus went:

> *Moustache Man, Moustache Man.*
> *Who will stop Moustache Man?*
> *And the GTC from over the sea*
> *That made him boss of you and me?*

Joe was still humming the catchy tune as they approached the town. It seemed to be as busy as Porto Pearls. They might have to question hundreds of people before they found out anything.

Ma asked a woman if she could recommend a hotel. She pointed up the hill and said that overseas visitors often stayed at the Falcon.

Every narrow building was painted a different colour, and many were patterned too. Francie laughed and clapped. Even Ma had never seen such tall and highly decorated buildings before. When she started explaining proportions and ratios, Joe stopped listening, although Sal and Francie seemed interested.

Just as it was getting dark, Humphrey pointed out an "H" for Humphrey and an "F" for Francie. Yes! The Falcon Hotel.

"Good spotting, Humph," said Joe.

Before they went inside, Ma spoke firmly to Carrot, who'd been riding on Sal's shoulder. "I don't imagine they like birds in this hotel, but we want to stay here, so you have a choice."

Carrot cocked her head.

"You can find a tree for a day or two, or play dead on my hat—no squawking, no moving. Understood?"

Carrot flew onto Ma's sunhat, tucked in her head and lay sprawled around the crown like a very expensive decoration.

"Good bird." Ma held her back straight and her head very upright as she climbed the steps.

Although the Falcon Hotel was grand, with thick carpet and marble pillars in the reception area, the woman at the desk was friendly. "Follow me please, madam? Your rooms are on floor five, but we have a cyclic ascender for the convenience of our guests. It's the only one in Cruxcia." She spoke differently from the people in Porto Pearls. "Cruxcia" sounded like "Crrrrrooosha".

The ascender beside the staircase consisted of a string of small open-sided cabins that moved continuously, going up on the left and down on the right. Joe looked at Francie. Fun or scary? And she looked back: fun!

"If you ascend with two children, madam, I will accompany the other two. Step in when I say, and step out at floor five. When the floor is level—now."

Ma stepped into the cabin with Humphrey and Francie, and

they rose slowly until they disappeared through the ceiling, though Joe could still hear Humph's gleeful squealing.

"Step now!"

Sal and Joe jumped in and turned to face the open front. They were being raised towards the fancy ceiling of the hotel lobby, then past the ceiling and the floor above with a "1" painted on it. There was the carpeted corridor, the doors and walls, then another ceiling. They were standing still and the hotel was slipping past them.

"I've read about these," said Sal. "Hydraulically powered. So clever."

"Be ready to step out," said the receptionist, "now."

They stepped out to join the others. Humphrey was jumping about in excitement. Ma was trying to be dignified but she couldn't help smiling.

The receptionist showed them to two adjoining bedrooms and called Humphrey "Little Pumpkin", which made Joe and Francie giggle. As soon as she had gone, Ma opened the window, which looked out on the stables at the back of the hotel, and told Carrot that she could go and explore while they were at the restaurant for dinner.

Ma made Humphrey have a proper wash, then she turned to Joe. "You must have a cleaner shirt, and Sal, you look like one of those Porto Pearls urchins. For goodness' sake, brush your hair."

Sal began quietly. "No one would believe that the four of us survived a month without adults." She yanked the string off her plaits and ran her fingers through the tangles. "No one would think that we crossed mountains and rivers. Without adults."

She brushed hard and got louder. "No one would think that we won the money that's paying for this expedition. Without adults. Or a hairbrush." She re-plaited fast. "No one would think that we are responsible and sensible, the way you constantly tell us what to do. As if we're babies!" That was pretty loud.

Francie winced, but Ma smiled at Sal and gave her a quick hug. "You look beautiful."

Then they squashed into a descending cabin and floated down to the restaurant. The waiter looked at the family as if a bunch of elephants had come to cause chaos in his orderly dining room, and led them to an alcove overlooking the street, tucked out of sight of the other diners. He lit the lamp over their table and handed them each a menu.

"Oh dear. I can't read this curly writing, and I don't even know what language it's in. Let's each pick something and share," suggested Ma.

It turned out that Sal had chosen green soup, and Humphrey a plump fish with yellow sauce. Francie had picked a whole roast chicken with roast potatoes and purple vegetables, and Ma a bowl of slippery little dumplings. Joe was starving. The waiter put a small plate of salad in front of him, sprinkled with something like fried worms.

"Francie wins by miles!"

Ma cut up the chicken and shared everything out, except the salad, which no one wanted to try.

"That fish was nearly as yummy as the ones Beckett caught," said Humph when they'd finished.

"I miss Beckett," said Joe. "I liked having a big brother."

There was a racket of voices outside and Joe cupped his hands around his eyes to see out the window. Men were approaching the front door of the hotel.

Then the waiter glided up to their table pushing a trolley laden with desserts.

"Crikeyomikey, I hope we stay here for a year," said Joe.

With all that choice, Ma asked for a plate of cheese. Sal chose a meringue cake oozing with cream and berries. Francie pointed to a slice of shiny chocolate tart, Humphrey went for a pink cake with yellow icing, and Joe chose a chocolate log. They swapped spoonsful, and agreed that all were equally delicious.

They were just running their fingers over their empty plates when they heard a familiar voice. Joe and Francie exchanged horrified glances and Joe slipped out of his seat and peered around the alcove. A giant. Coming into the dining room.

Joe slid back, unseen. "It's him! It's Cody Cole!"

Chapter Three

Cowboys

"No! Don't let him see us," Sal hissed.

Ma was rigid. "Cody Cole? The man who kidnapped Humphrey on the Great Race?" She gripped her cheese knife and looked ready to chop the leader of the Cowboys up like the chicken.

Humph slid under the table and Francie sat frozen.

"Stay here all of you," Ma said, "I'm going to have a word with that man."

Sal gripped her arm. "No, you mustn't, Ma, please no. You don't know how dangerous he is."

The men's voices were booming across the dining room. "Less than a week to go!" said one.

"What a good day," said another. "You should've seen that woman's face when the Custodians caught her."

Panic washed over Sal. She couldn't think straight, but she knew one thing for sure. "They mustn't know we're here."

"That'll be the last of the troublemakers." Cody Cole's voice was unmistakeable. "I hope they're kept in prison until their hair falls out."

The men roared with nasty laughter.

"All right, I won't speak to him." Ma lifted Humphrey onto her lap. "He can't hurt you, we'll keep you safe," she whispered. "What are they doing, Sal?"

Sal peeked around the alcove. "The waiter's giving them menus and lighting their lamp. It's very bright. Turn our lamp off, Joe. If we slip out now, they won't see us."

"Ready?" whispered Ma. "Stick together."

Humphrey clung to her front like a baby monkey, and they slid, ghostly ghosts, out of the dining room and into the ascender. They collapsed in a heap on Ma's bed. Humph was terrified that the Cowboys would come for him in the night, but Ma showed him the locked doors and promised they'd find somewhere else to stay tomorrow.

"I really need a story," Humph pleaded when he was in bed.

Ma sat up beside him with a pillow at her back. "When I was not much older than you, I lived with my mother, father and brothers in a big city. But one day my oldest brother got sick, so I was sent away to the country to stay with my great-aunt and uncle. They were mapmakers—retired by then—who'd once been explorers. They lived in a little house by a lake. For the first time I explored outside without a grown-up. I climbed trees and splashed in the lake and made pots from clay that I mined from the bank of the stream, and I didn't have to go to school. It was paradise.

"My great-uncle took me for long walks and told me the names of trees, and how to read the weather. My great-aunt told me stories, and taught me to measure and calculate, but the main thing we did was draw maps together. She never said, but I think she could fly, like Francie. We mapped the village, then started on…"

While Ma talked, Sal doodled in her notebook, making rows of dots and connecting them with straight lines to make curves. It helped her think.

"They had a dog called Ticky who could…"

Humph's eyes closed and his thumb slipped out of his mouth. Ma pulled her arm out from under his head and pulled the cover over him. "More tales of my youth another night."

Joe was lounging across the foot of the bed, feeding Carrot bits of salad that he'd saved from dinner. "Say 'Joe'."

"Go," said Carrot.

"Close enough. Have a worm-thing."

"What d'you think the Cowboys are doing here?" Sal asked.

"They must be on a job," said Ma. "Making a map, perhaps."

"I bet it's got something to do with Pa," said Sal. "The map, I mean."

Francie was drawing. She nodded.

"I bet that, too," said Joe.

"But what? What could it mean?" Sal pulled her boots off and yawned. "I'll think about it tomorrow. I could sleep for a week."

They left the door between the bedrooms open. In spite of her tiredness, Sal lay awake long after everyone else, listening to Ma snoring quietly in the other room. The last door down the hallway had opened and shut and the last voice disappeared down the road and still she lay there, thinking about the Cowboys. She remembered how she'd felt when she'd realised Humphrey was missing. Of course Ma wanted to shout at Cody Cole, but he'd take revenge. A faraway clock chimed eleven, then twelve.

In the morning they ate breakfast in their rooms. "Are we stuck here now?" Sal asked Ma quietly so Humphrey couldn't hear. "If we go out, Cody Cole might see us."

"He won't. I woke up early and saw the Cowboys take their horses, loaded up with all their equipment. The cook came out and gave Cody Cole a food hamper. It looks as if they plan to be away for a while. We're safe to go out and get our bearings, but this town is such a maze, I think we need help. The receptionist said she'd find a guide for us."

After they'd walked a couple of streets, Sal stopped worrying that they might see the Cowboys around every corner. Cruxcia wasn't as big as Porto Pearls, but it was just as busy. Lots of the buildings had shops at ground level, often a whole row selling the same thing, their displays spilling out onto the street. On one road every shop sold fabrics, and Francie paused to run her fingers over the colours. A couple of streets later, every shop made and sold sandals.

People passing in the street or chatting in doorways turned to look at them.

"They're all staring at me," said Humph. "I don't like it."

"Nor does Francie," said Joe.

"I think they're just curious," said Sal. "No one else is dressed like us."

Cruxcians all wore brightly coloured long, loose tops and trousers, with sandals, but the Santanders wore knee-length wool trousers, socks, boots and flannel shirts.

"I promise I'll buy us all Cruxcian clothes when I've changed some coins for local money," said Ma. "Now let's see if your route-finding skills can lead us back to the Falcon, Joe."

"This way," said Joe and dived down an alley Sal was sure they hadn't come up. They followed and were back at the hotel in no time.

They'd just finished packing up their bags when a woman and a girl about Joe and Francie's age appeared at their door.

"Shala. My name is Tash Terrabynd, citizen of Cruxcia, daughter of Clarrie, wife of Taliesin," the woman announced. "Member of the Society of Guides and Interpreters."

"And my name is Hessa, citizen of Cruxcia," said the girl. "Daughter of Tash and Taliesin. Shala—that's Cruxcian for 'hello'."

Tash was tall and frowny, whereas Hessa was smiley with dimples. Her masses of curly black hair were held back by an orange scarf, and she looked around like someone who found everything curious and most things hilarious.

Ma introduced everyone the usual way, then Tash showed them the Cruxcian way. "You take the other person's hand and touch it to your forehead, and you say your name. Then the other person takes your hand to their forehead."

Sal thought of all the Cruxcian ways she might need to know, and how easy it would be to do the wrong thing.

"That's just for formal," said Hessa (who rolled her r's just like the receptionist). "Mostly we just go—" She touched her forehead with her middle fingers then directed her hand, palm up, at the person she was greeting. That looked much easier.

The adults took the two chairs and the children sat on the beds and listened.

"Sit straight!" Carrot ordered from the window ledge, and everyone sat straighter, then laughed. Carrot flew down to Sal's wrist, and Ma introduced her, too. "Carrot learned to talk by listening to a bossy teacher. I'm sorry, she's sometimes rather rude," said Ma.

"You're rude," said Carrot.

Ma explained that they were looking for her husband, Leopold Santander, the children's father. Sal noticed Tash and Hessa stiffen at his name. They'd heard of him before. She felt a lurch of hope, but Ma didn't seem to have noticed.

Ma told Tash how they had followed Pa's trail to Cruxcia. "I believe that my husband and Waldo Watkins were part of a team employed by one Zander Abercrombie, to explore and map in this region. We've come to find out where he is."

"You need someone to make enquiries for you?" asked Tash.

"And help us find our way around," said Ma.

Sal stroked Carrot's back. "Tell about Cody Cole, Ma."

"He's a bad man," whispered Humphrey. He put his thumb in his mouth and buried his face in Francie's tummy.

Ma told Tash about seeing the Cowboys' mapmaking team last night.

"We competed against him in a mapping race," said Sal. "He and the rest of the Cowboys are cruel, and they cheat. We need to avoid them at any cost."

"We know a bit about the Cowboys, and we also try to avoid them," said Tash. "I think the first thing you need is a safe hotel."

Ma nodded. "Thank you. How do you say that in Cruxcia?"

"Dasa," smiled Tash.

Tash and Hessa went down in the first descending cabin. When Sal and Joe hopped out of the next cabin, Tash and Hessa were talking urgently. Sal distinctly heard "Cowboys", "Santander" and "Cody Cole". Tash shook her head and pressed her lips together when Sal came towards them, and Hessa rolled her eyes.

Surely an eye roll meant the same in all cultures.

Chapter Four

How Humphrey Saved the Day

They followed Tash down a narrow lane, which led higgledy-piggledy into an even narrower alley with barely room for two people to walk side by side. There were posters stuck on the walls with red writing and a picture of a Cruxcian building.

"Freedom for Cruxcia, freedom for Cruxcians," Joe read. "Freedom from what?"

"The GTC and Governor Mundle," said Hessa.

"Who's that?

"He's like the ruler of Cruxcia. We hate him," said Hessa.

The alley became several flights of ascending steps, and they were panting when they emerged into a wide, open square with shade trees and bench seats around the edges. They put their bags down for a minute.

"This is the top, the centre of the town," said Tash. "The old building over there is the Societies' Meeting Hall. There are concerts and dances here in the square sometimes. Or there used to be."

In the middle of the square, two workmen were trowelling cement around the plinth of a larger-than-life statue of a man who stared out over everyone's heads. His high-plumed hat made him look even taller, and an enormously long moustache spiralled out from his cheeks and pointed at them. Underneath was a plaque:

> WITH BOUNDLESS ADMIRATION
> FOR OUR GLORIOUS GOVERNOR
> HIS EXCELLENCY MALVICIOUS MUNDLE
> FROM THE GRATEFUL PEOPLE OF CRUXCIA

"What's it say?" asked Humphrey.

Joe read the words to him.

"What's that mean?" asked Humph.

"I've no idea," said Joe. "Moustache Man, Moustache Man." He started singing, but Tash shook her head at him and glanced round, checking for—what?

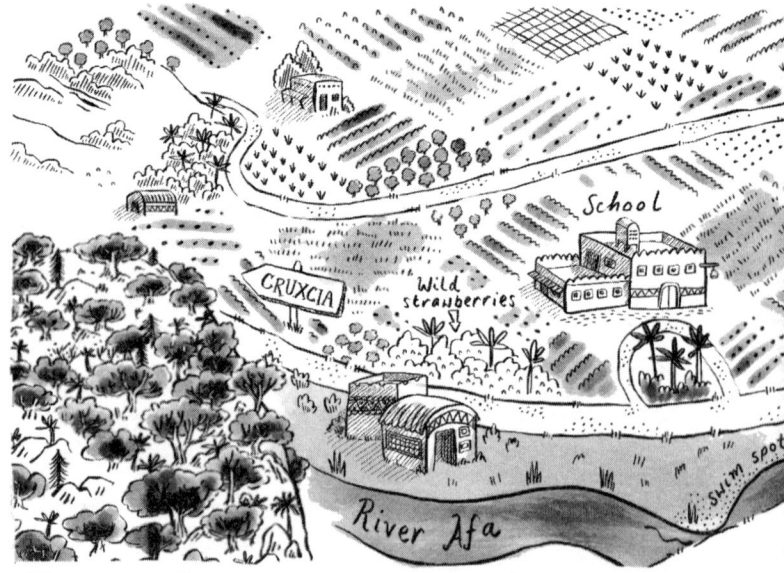

"This statue is new." She spoke quietly. "From the grateful people of Cruxcia indeed! He commissioned it himself, but I doubt the sculptor will get paid. I suppose the town's pigeons will enjoy sitting on him."

Carrot fluttered onto the plume of His Excellency's hat and deposited a white streak on it. The workmen laughed.

They stopped at the corner to cross a busy street. Tash, Sal, Ma and Humphrey darted through the flow of ox carts, horse carts and donkeys but Joe, Francie and Hessa weren't as fast.

"Wow, so busy!" said Joe.

"Don't you have traffic where you come from?" asked Hessa. "Where *do* you come from?"

That was a tricky question. "Just now we came by boat from New Coalhaven to Porto Pearls, and then in a dirigible. But we didn't live in New Coalhaven. We don't come from anywhere, really. Mapmaking families move around a lot. But we lived in our last house for nearly a year."

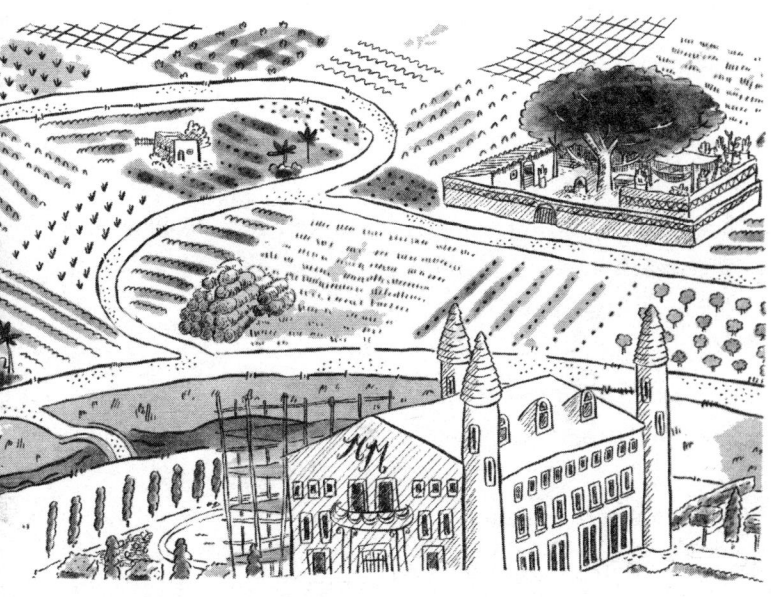

"Not even a year! How do you keep friends?" asked Hessa.

A blast of noise saved Joe from answering that he had no friends, apart from his family, and Beckett, who lived many weeks' journey away. A uniformed man on horseback was blowing a horn to clear the road ahead of a procession. Behind him came a maroon roofless carriage with twirly gold decorations, pulled by four white horses. A driver and footman sat up the front, and in the back, a man in a top hat with a moustache that corkscrewed out from his cheeks. Facing him were a short man and a very tall woman. The woman turned and stared at Francie and Joe, nudged the man and pointed.

"It's him—the governor—Moustache-Man Mundle!" Hessa hissed.

"Do you know the other two?"

Hessa shook her head. "No idea."

Behind Mundle's carriage came another carrying six men and women, all wearing jewels that flashed in the sun.

"They look as though they're going to a ball," said Joe.

"We call them the mumazus—a kind of toad that hangs on to a cow's tail," said Hessa. "They're Mundle's hangers-on. He buys them things and they tell him how wonderful he is."

A lot of people had stopped to watch the governor go past, or maybe they were just waiting to cross the road. An old woman near Hessa shouted, "Give me back my son, you evil man!" and shook her fist at Moustache Man.

He saw, and shouted, "Seize her!"

Two of the maroon-uniformed men following on horseback dismounted. They strode towards the woman. No one spoke or even looked at her, but suddenly the roadside crowd moved together like a flock of birds or a shoal of fish and Joe, Francie and Hessa found themselves part of it. Whichever way the uniformed men moved, the protective flock moved too, until the woman was out of sight.

"What just happened?" asked Joe.

"She got saved from the Custodians, who would have arrested her."

"But she didn't do anything!" Joe felt his face get hot and tight.

Hessa, Joe and Francie crossed the road and ran to catch up with the others, who were turning into a narrow side street.

"Tash! Wait," Hessa shouted. "We just saw Mundle. They tried to arrest an old woman who yelled at him."

"What happened?"

"We all got in their way."

"Good." Tash looked around and put her finger to her lips. Hessa nodded.

"Tall and Short were in the carriage with Moustache Man," said Joe quietly. "And they saw us."

"Uh-oh," said Sal. "That gives me a really bad feeling."

What did it mean that Tall and Short were with Governor Mundle? And what kind of place was this, where you could get arrested for shaking your fist?

They turned into a quiet lane.

"This town is a maze," Sal said to Joe. "I'd be happier if we knew of any hidey-holes, like Ma said. Are you learning our route?"

Joe nodded. He didn't have Sal's special maths talent or Francie's drawing talent, but he prided himself on knowing where he was. Since the Great Race he'd found he could tell north, even blindfolded. Ma said he'd built a compass into his brain, like a migrating bird.

Knowing which way was north didn't help in such a confusion of alleys and lanes, but as soon as he'd fixed the pattern of the main streets of Cruxcia in his head, he'd be able to find his way anywhere. Though he hoped he didn't have to. More than anything he wanted to be route-finding with Pa again in the mountains.

"If you're lost or want to know where something is in Cruxcia, always ask a child," said Hessa. "We all know our own quarter better than the adults. We earn coins delivering messages and showing people where someone lives, or where something is."

"Horses coming! Off the road," Tash called. Two men in the same maroon and gold uniforms were cantering up the lane. "I don't believe it," she muttered. "Custodians. What can they want?"

The Custodians halted and dismounted. Joe's heart was thumping in his throat and he could feel Francie's fear. He grabbed her hand and stood in front of her. One man barked, "Stop where you are! I am Lieutenant Loofus." He had four gold stripes on his sleeves, a plumed helmet, a silver buckle engraved with GTC, and on his belt a curved sword and a pistol. "I wish to know the contents of your bags. Search them, Private Clocksley."

Carrot flew around Private Clocksley's head screeching, "Tick-tock, tick-tock."

"Control that bird!" demanded Loofus, drawing his pistol.

Joe whistled for Carrot and she sat on his finger, quivering.

Private Clocksley (one stripe, no plume, no sword or pistol) tipped the tools out of the tool bag and stirred them with his truncheon.

Lieutenant Loofus kicked the theodolite with the toe of his shiny boot. "And what would this be?"

"It's a theodolite. The tools are for surveying." Ma was trying hard to hide her anger. "We're mapmakers. We're visiting."

Loofus looked at her sharply. "You admit to that, do you? Well, well, well. Your name?"

"Angelica Santander."

"Write that down, Private Clocksley."

The private hung the truncheon from his belt and took a tiny notebook and miniature pencil from his chest pocket.

Lieutenant Loofus asked Tash for her name, then demanded to know where the visitors were staying.

Tash answered. "The Grand View Hotel. Sir."

"We'll escort you there," said Loofus, "in order to conduct a more thorough search, and ask you further questions."

Just then, Humphrey, who had been unusually quiet all morning, turned pale, moaned, and was sick. Spectacularly sick. First, vomit only flecked his legs, but another surge came, and another, which splashed the Custodians' trousers and doused their boots. It also made an impressive puddle between them, which they kept treading in as they tried to get out of the way. Joe saw remnants of today's breakfast, and traces of last night's pink cake with yellow icing. Also, quite a lot of carrot, which was odd as they hadn't eaten carrots for ages.

Everyone held their noses, except Humphrey.

"That is disgusting! Abominable!" Lieutenant Loofus's face was beetroot-coloured. "We will return to barracks to clean off this noxious mess, but we will not be diverted. You will go to the Grand View Hotel immediately and remain there until we come. Then you will answer our questions."

"Sorry, sorry," sobbed Humph, as the men got back on their horses and cantered away.

Joe helped Sal put the tools back into the bag and Ma found a cloth to wipe the sick off Humph. She put a hand to his forehead. "He's feverish. I'll carry him."

An old man who'd been watching from his doorway called out, "You get going, quick. I'll fetch sawdust for the mess."

Tash thanked him, and picked up Ma's heavy carpetbag. "Those Custodians are trouble." She strode off up the lane.

"But they're coming to the hotel," said Sal.

"We won't be there," said Tash. "Well done, Humphrey, I know you must feel horrible but I think you've just saved the day."

"Why, what—?" Ma began. But then she just said, "Thank you," and followed.

Tash said, "We'll take him to Pi's, Hessa."

"What's Pi's?" Joe whispered.

"Pi is Tash's sister. She's an apothecary and a nurse, and she runs an infirmary."

They walked fast. Humphrey's eyes were closed and his head hung limp on Ma's shoulder. His skin was pale and clammy and although he was barely conscious, he kept groaning.

Tash turned into a shop with a wall lined with glass bottles full of brightly coloured liquids, and another wall full of tiny drawers. It smelled of cloves and lemons. A passage led to a door, then they were in a cool room with sofas and low tables and Tash was calling for her sister.

A tall woman appeared from a back room. She was bony and angular, not like Joe's cuddly image of a nurse. "Tash, Hessa, shala. What brings you here?" She went to hug them, then noticed Ma with Humphrey and pulled out a chair instead. She felt Humphrey's forehead and held his wrist.

Then Ma started to sway. Tash caught her as she slumped sideways, groaning and clutching her stomach.

Pi lifted Humphrey off Ma and laid him on a sofa while Hessa grabbed a bowl of rose petals from the table, tipped them out and held it for Ma to be sick into. When she'd finished vomiting, the two women half-carried Ma through to a bedroom. Tash came back and scooped up Humphrey, and closed the door behind them.

Francie made little grunting noises and her fear pulsed into Joe. Ma was never sick. Never ever. He squeezed Francie's hand tight and they sat in petrified silence. Joe looked at Sal. Ma sick? "Now what?" he whispered.

Sal pinched her lips together and shook her head.

After a while Pi came out to talk to them. "Do any of you feel ill?"

Sal, Francie and Joe all felt fine.

"Did your mother and brother eat or drink anything different from you yesterday?"

Sal looked at Joe. "We all had the same things, didn't we?"

"We shared our whole dinner," said Joe. "Except for Ma's cheese."

Francie took her drawing pad from her rucksack and her pencil out of her hair. She drew rapidly. Joe peered over her shoulder. The market—drinking.

"Francie's right! At the market yesterday, we had fresh coconuts, but they both had an iced lemon drink with mint."

Pi spoke fast while she tied on a clean apron. "That'll be it. Sometimes there's bad water in the ice. The sickness may pass quickly or it may take some days. I'll mix up some medicine and look after them here."

"Don't look so worried!" said Tash, coming into the room. "They'll be better in no time. You three go home with Hessa—you can stay with us. I've got some things to do but I'll come and see how they are before I come home."

"Dasa. Thank you," said Sal. "That's so kind of you."

Sal's elbow dug into Joe's ribs. What? "Oh, yes, dasa," he said, flustered.

They tiptoed in to kiss Ma and Humphrey, who were side by side in a low bed, as pale and still as stone carvings. Joe looked closely to make sure that their chests were still going up and down. Ma's carpetbag was extremely heavy. Joe and Sal had to keep changing hands, and his heart sank when Hessa said they lived half an hour up the valley. Luckily, they hadn't walked far when a boy stopped his horse and cart for them. They scrambled up onto the back, which was half full of crates and sacks.

"Thanks, Stracky," said Hessa. "Stracky lives on the farm next to us. He's only ten but he can turn the horse and cart in our lane, which none of his brothers can do. This is Sal, Joe and Francie. They come from overseas."

"Hello, visitors!" Stracky turned and touched his forehead beneath a mop of sticking-up hair. They all returned the Cruxcian greeting.

"I'm stopping at your place anyway. The crate's for you."

Carrot fluttered onto a crate and pecked curiously at it. "Hello bird? Hello bird?"

"I'm afraid they only speak pigeon, Carrot. Carrroo, carrrooo," said Hessa.

"Pigeons in a box!" Carrot sounded more gleeful than sorry.

The road ran alongside the River Afa. Across the Afa was the tree-covered hill that they'd seen from the dirigible and in Waldo Watkin's picture.

"That," said Hessa, "is Mina Mendalwar, our special place where everyone is buried when they die. It's been our burying place for over five hundred years. My great-grandmother, and my great-great-grandfather—all the greats are in the hill."

Joe tried to imagine living in a place where your ancestors had lived. He didn't even know who his ancestors were. Their grandparents were dead and Ma's brothers had been killed in a faraway war, so they had no relations, as far as he knew.

"It's the Hallowmas Festival soon and we have fireworks over there on Hallowmas Eve." Hessa pointed to the grassy bank between the river and the hill. "It's one of the best days of the year."

High above the river, in a fold of the valley, was an enormous building all by itself. It was still being built, with scaffolding on one side. It didn't look very Cruxcian because it was wide, with turrets like a fairytale castle and lots of windows. There were gardens on either side and a lawn in front.

"That's Moustache Man's mansion," said Hessa. And when she said "Moustache Man", she and Stracky both pretended to spit onto the road.

"It must have fifty bedrooms," said Sal.

"For all Mundle's mumazus," said Hessa.

Hessa and Stracky pointed out other sights. A great place for picking wild strawberries, the best summer swimming place, and their school (though the Harvest Holiday had just started).

"We've never been to school," said Joe. "Ma teaches us because we move around so much. Francie and I don't mind, but Sal wants to go to school more than anything."

Sal nodded. "True. And I will one day."

Stracky turned the cart down a lane beside a field with an enormous stack of hay bales in one corner, and he stopped at a purple gate in an orange wall. They followed Hessa into a courtyard with a very wide tree in the middle, with a fireplace, table and benches in its shade. There were shelves with pots and crockery next to the fireplace, like an outdoor kitchen. A pink, single-storey house with a flat roof stood on one side of the courtyard, and outbuildings (painted yellow with purple doors) along the other. The orange wall was the third side and the fourth was a low red wall leading to an orchard and vegetable garden.

Joe stared round. "Wow. Is this a farm?"

"Not really," said Hessa, "though we have sheep up the valley and we make hay every year."

They piled all their belongings, and the crate, under the tree. Carrot flew onto Francie's shoulder and squawked. In response, an eerie shriek came from one of the sheds, making the hairs on Joe's arms prickle. Carrot squealed and tried to hide under Francie's hair.

"That was only Magnus saying hello," said Hessa. "I'll introduce you later. Come in and meet Vivi."

"Stay here, Carrot," said Joe.

It was cool and dark in the main room of the house. Joe couldn't make out anything until his eyes adjusted. Then it seemed dazzling: the floor and some of the walls were covered with brightly patterned rugs. It was like stepping inside a kaleidoscope. A girl was sitting at a table in a chair that had a large wheel either side of the seat and two tiny wheels in front. Joe had never seen anything like it before. She had a ginger cat on her lap and she was surrounded by books and papers.

"This is my sister Vivi, and the cat's Hercules. They're both nearly eighteen. How old are you?"

"Sal's fourteen and we're twelve," said Joe.

"Same as me! Vivi, this is Sal, Joe and Francie."

Vivi touched her forehead. Hercules jumped down and stalked straight over to Francie. She held her hand out and he sniffed her fingers and began to purr.

"He likes you. Usually he is—what's the word?" Hessa stuck her nose in the air and squeezed up her mouth.

"Stuck-up?" said Joe.

"Supercilious," said Vivi.

"Vivi spends all her time studying," said Hessa. "Crazy girl!"

Joe couldn't help glancing down. Vivi's legs were covered by trousers but her feet looked normal.

Hessa poked around in a cupboard. "They're staying with us

and Tash said to feed them. Can we eat your sunderstrum?"

"If you keep the stickiness away from my papers. Let's go outside."

Hessa took a tin from the shelf. "Also, the Custodians are after them—and Stracky's brought the pigeons."

Vivi propelled her chair expertly through the hens, and over to the table under the tree. "So what's the story?"

Hessa explained about Ma and Humphrey being sick at Auntie Pi's house while Joe concentrated on the sunderstrum, which turned out to be small honey and almond cakes. He hoped Hessa would offer him another one, but she was busy telling Vivi about the Custodians and how interested they were in Ma's tool bag.

"Why did you come to Cruxcia?" asked Vivi.

"To find our father," said Sal. "He's a mapmaker who came here a year ago and never came home. We got here yesterday. And then we found out there were other mapmakers in our hotel called Cody Cole and his Cowboys. They're bad people. Evil. Then we met your mother and Hessa, to be our guides and find us a new hotel and help us look for Pa, then Ma and our little brother got sick and now your Auntie Pi is looking after them and that's why we're here."

Vivi listened and nodded. Then she asked, "Your father. Is his name Leopold Santander?"

Chapter Five

A Lot of "Whys?" and Some "Becauses"

"Why?" Sal felt suddenly desperate. "What do you know?" She stopped breathing.

"Your father was arrested. He's in the prison."

"Alive!" Joe, Francie and Sal jumped up and hugged each other and squealed, "Alive, alive, alive!"

But in prison. They stopped jumping around. Sal and Joe bombarded Vivi with questions. Why was he arrested? What for? What happened? Was he all right? Did Tash know? Why hadn't she said so?

Carrot landed on the table and strutted up and down squawking, "Cock-a-doodle-do! What? Why? Who?"

Hessa stroked Carrot's head. "It's not only him. Our father's in prison, and our uncle and aunt—lots and lots of people. Most without a trial. We haven't seen our papa for weeks."

Sal stared from Hessa to Vivi. "All in prison?"

Vivi nodded. "I'll try and explain, but it's a bit complicated."

They sat down again to listen. Sal sucked the end of her plait.

"A few years ago, the GTC appointed Mundle to be our governor. To rule us," said Vivi. "Last year, he employed your father's mapmaking team to come here secretly and make some maps. When the Town Council found out what they were doing, they asked them to stop mapping, so they did.

"That made Moustache Man very angry and he sent Custodians to arrest the mapmakers. The others escaped but your father was caught. They accused him of breaking his contract and put him in prison."

Sal flicked away the plait. "But why did the Council want them to stop mapping?" There was a stone inside her and she was leaking tears. Francie gave Sal her hankie and leaned against her.

"Because of what Moustache Man wanted them for."

Joe frowned. "What did he want them for?"

A chicken fluttered onto the table. "We don't know. Get off." Hessa pushed it off.

"Arghhhh!" Sal slumped down. "I don't understand."

Hessa patted her arm. "We don't know exactly why he wants maps, but it must be something bad because he's the one who wants them. We think he means to take over our farms, or dig up our valley for coal mines."

"What?" Sal remembered the valley near Coalhaven, choked in filthy coal dust. "That's terrible!"

Vivi nodded. "Did you come in a dirigible?"

"Yes, it was the best ever!" said Joe.

"Did you notice our sacred hill, Mina Mendalwar, as you were flying in, and this valley and the River Afa and the mountains covered in forest? It all belongs to the people of Cruxcia. *All* the people. The valley is where most of our food is grown, we get our wood from the forest, and Mina Mendalwar is where our ancestors lie. And that's where they were mapping."

Sal tried to imagine this beautiful valley being dug up. She couldn't. Her fingers absent-mindedly squished up the cake crumbs from the table and popped them into her mouth. "But maybe the maps were just for knowledge?"

Vivi shook her head. "No. We've got maps. Mundle is one of the meanest and greediest men on this planet. He wouldn't spend a bean unless he was sure of getting a whole bean farm in exchange. If he has a secret plan, and he's paying people actual money, then he's expecting to get very, very rich from it."

"Vivi's going to be a lawyer," said Hessa proudly. "You can tell, can't you?"

Sal nodded. "So, did you ever talk to our father?"

"Me?" Vivi frowned. "No. Just people from the Town Council. Who are mostly in prison now, but the others still don't invite me to their planning meetings. Idiots. But I'll show them. They will beg me to join the Council when I save Cruxcia."

Vivi took another cake and passed the tin round.

Sal exchanged a look with Joe that asked, is she really clever or does she just think she's clever? Francie had her head down. She was drawing chickens, but she was listening.

"Is that why Cody Cole's Cowboys are here—to do the job that Pa and Waldo Watkins's team were supposed to do?" said Sal.

"I'm sure it is. They've been mapping the valley for a while and people have been trying to stop them, which is partly why so many have been arrested," said Vivi.

"The Cowboys take Custodians with them now," said Hessa. "When Stracky's brother was driving their goats up the lane and they were coming down, they said he was deliberately obstructing them, and the Custodians arrested him."

"No!" said Sal. "A few months ago we entered a mapmaking race they were in. They cheated, and lied, and they even kidnapped Humphrey to stop us winning."

"What happened?" said Hessa.

"We got him back, and we won. They tried to steal the gold but we won it all in the end—that's how come we're here. We needed the winnings to search for Pa."

"You mapped a route, just you four children and your mother?"

"Not our mother—we lost each other before the race began. It was just us four and Beckett, a boy we met." Sal felt good being able to say that to someone like Vivi.

Vivi leaned forward. "You four are mapmakers, too? Not just your parents?"

Sal nodded. "I calculate and measure, Joe finds the route and Francie draws. It was a long race. Twenty-seven days."

"Oh thank you, ancestors," Vivi smiled up at the sky and the tree. Then she spun her wheelchair round. "Shhh, who's that?" She started propelling herself towards the house. Now Sal could hear horses, and male voices in the lane. "Custodians," Vivi said quietly. "Hide the Santanders, Hessa, quick."

"Oh no, oh help!" Hessa looked round frantically, then pointed at a door. "In the shed, take your bags."

"Carrot, hide in the tree. Quiet," Sal ordered. Carrot did as she was told.

The shed was dark, with just one small, very dirty window.

"Under the shelf—under the sacks," said Hessa.

They scrambled over to the workbench at the back of the shed and burrowed beneath a mound of empty sacks. Hessa threw more sacks on top. They smelled of dust and earth.

"Maybe they'll just go past," whispered Joe.

Sal twitched the sack away from her eyes enough to peek out. Hessa was looking through the window, then she jumped back out of sight. "They've come into the yard!"

Francie's fingers found Sal's wrist.

They heard heavy footsteps, then a voice bellowed. "Are your parents home, girlie?"

A babyish voice replied, "No." It didn't sound at all like Vivi.

"We're looking for Angelica Santander. Do you know her?"

Vivi's baby voice said, "No," then she cried, "Go away. Not in house!"

"And who's going to stop me? You?" Cruel laughter followed, and boots clomping across the yard.

"One's checking the roof. The other one's gone inside. It's the same ones Humphrey was sick on! Now they're both searching the house," said Hessa. "They didn't even take their boots off."

It only took a minute for the Custodians to satisfy themselves that no one was in, or on, the house. Then the boots clomped towards the sheds, starting at the far end of the yard.

"Don't move," whispered Hessa. Sal could see her silhouette lean towards something on a stand.

As the Custodians crowded through the doorway, Hessa pulled away a cloth; there was something alive underneath it. A head stretched up. Wings opened. It was a bird! A huge bird that seemed to fill the shed. It flapped its wings a couple of times and shrieked. The men tumbled backwards out of the door.

Sal whispered what she'd seen to Francie and Joe, and how beautiful the bird looked. They stayed, hardly breathing, until Vivi called that the men had gone and they could come out.

"I wonder why they're so desperate to find your mother," said Vivi.

Hessa laughed. "They probably want to make her pay for new boots!" She explained to Vivi what had happened when they met Loofus and Clocksley earlier.

"If you've got to throw up, you couldn't do it on more deserving feet!" said Vivi.

The bird was a hunting hawk called Magnus. Hessa pulled on a thick leather gauntlet and brought him out into the yard, and Vivi rewarded him with a piece of raw meat. Carrot flew onto Sal's shoulder and shivered. Sal introduced her to Magnus, who stood like an aloof king on the arm of Vivi's chair. Even with his wings folded he was an imposing figure. Carrot bowed her head three times. "Your high, high, high-ty-ness."

Francie was enchanted and drew Magnus's hooked beak, unblinking yellow eyes and the pattern of his feathers.

Hessa and Vivi had trained Magnus themselves. They'd learned from an elderly falconer in the valley, and now Magnus sometimes caught rabbits for Hessa. "Which we eat a lot, like tonight." Hessa lit the outdoor fire and put on a pot of rabbit stew to heat up, then she said, "Please don't tell Tash that we told you about your father. She told me not to. I don't know why."

"She probably wanted to check you out first," said Vivi. "Mundle has spies. She's not sure who we can trust. And she's on the Town Council so I bet she thinks they need to have a meeting about you before she tells you anything."

"Or maybe she wanted to talk to your mother alone," said Hessa, "with no children listening. She's like that, never bursts out with things."

"She'll be too tired for much chat when she gets home anyway," said Vivi.

"Why?" asked Joe. "What's she been doing?"

Hessa put bowls and cutlery on the table. "Tash does lots of things. Her paid work is as a guide. Her second work is with Taliesin, our father, in his paint workshop, but not while he's in prison. Her third work—which is all our work—is the garden, growing food. But her main task now is with the Town Council. A lot of people have been arrested, and she's the person who visits their children. 'Are you all right? Have you eaten dinner? Did you brush your teeth?'—all that. All day, every day, unless she gets paid work guiding visitors."

It was dark, and the rabbit stew had been smelling tantalising for some time when Tash came through the gate. While they ate, Tash reassured them that Auntie Pi was the best person in Cruxcia for looking after the sick. Then they told Tash about the visit from the Custodians.

"They were looking for Angelica, but they asked about you. They know you live here," said Vivi.

"You did well," said Tash. "Good idea to hide."

"Are the Custodians actual soldiers?" asked Sal.

"Not exactly," said Tash. "Cruxcia hasn't got an army. The Custodians work for the Grania Trading Company, who claimed they needed armed guards to protect their ornithopters and dirigibles. Then they started imposing new taxes and rules on us, and appointed Mundle as governor." Tash started piling up their empty bowls and spoons. "We weren't happy about that so they brought in more Custodians to ensure we obey. But the rules are unfair and the Custodians are unfair. Mundle and his supporters are getting rich while we're finding it harder to make a penny go round."

It was pitch black beyond the circle of light from the lantern and the glow of the embers in the fire. Sal couldn't help yawning.

"Bedtime for travellers," said Tash. "Off you go. I'll do the dishes tonight. And don't worry. Your mother and brother will be better soon, and you're welcome to stay here for as long as you want."

Bed was up the flight of outside steps that led to the house's flat roof. There was a hammock under an awning, a roll of sleeping pads, and a pile of pillows and quilts in a box.

"I'll sleep up here, too," said Hessa, "to keep you company."

Sal lay in her sleeping bag, which still smelled of the ocean from the nights at sea on the way to Porto Pearls. She was exhausted, but once again she couldn't sleep. She was worried that she had forgotten something. Something important. Maps ... altimeter and theodolite … safe in the shed. Ma and Humph? … safe as they could be at Auntie Pi's. Francie? … sleeping beside her, making little snuffling noises. Joe? … next to Francie. Carrot? … roosting on the edge of one of the plant pots that rimmed the roof. And Pa? … was alive! The prison might even be quite close by. It was only the fourth night since they'd got off the boat at Porto Pearls and already they'd found out where Pa was. Now they just had to get him out.

Why wasn't she asleep? She was finally drifting off when she jerked awake. Ma's purse! That's what she needed to remember. The horror of having no money for the Great Race and having to set off without proper supplies came flooding back. Tomorrow she'd put money into her Waldo purse. She could buy some food. Hessa had said that guiding was the only money Tash earned. Ma hadn't paid Tash and now she was looking after them as well as her own family. Sal had a purse and she was old enough to start paying for things.

Chapter Six

Progress and Progress

There were loud voices in the yard and Hessa's bed was empty. Joe peered over the edge of the roof between two pot plants. Breakfast things were piled on the outside table and Hessa was sitting at one end of it, crying. A woman was comforting her. Vivi was nearby; Joe could hear her voice, hard and angry. He shook Francie and Sal awake. "Something's happened."

Francie looked frightened. Sal sat up. "Is it Custodians?"

"I don't know. I can't hear any."

They went cautiously down the stairs. There were no Custodians, and the woman was just leaving. She squeezed Hessa's shoulder and touched her forehead to Vivi.

Hessa blew her nose and Vivi explained that the woman was their neighbour Ronia, Stracky's mother. She'd seen Tash being questioned by Custodians out on the road. When they'd led Tash away, she'd run to tell Vivi and Hessa.

"Tash was on her way to town to do her breakfast rounds. To make sure the children whose parents are in prison get fed," Vivi said bitterly.

It was Loofus and Clocksley who had arrested Tash. They'd accused her of evading arrest, because she hadn't taken the family to wait at the hotel as they'd told her to. And they accused her of concealing the whereabouts of a person of interest.

"They meant your mother. Your mother is *a person of interest*," Hessa said. "It sounds important." Her voice was wobbly.

"We've brought all this trouble on you—I'm really sorry," said Sal.

"It's not your fault," Hessa wailed. "We've been expecting them to arrest her for weeks."

Vivi nodded. "It's true." She swung her chair over to the fireplace where a kettle was boiling. "Come on Hessy-Bess, pass over the kafe jug and blow your nose. We've been practically orphans for weeks now, anyway."

"What about Ma?" asked Joe. "Do you think the Custodians will search Pi's?"

"They might. I'll send a pigeon to Lysander. He'll warn Auntie Pi," said Vivi.

Joe was relieved that Vivi knew what needed to be done next.

Vivi snorted an odd laugh. "Apparently, as Tash was being led away, she said, *Tell the girls I love them and there's a list of all the urgent jobs on the pantry shelf.* As if we didn't have enough to do."

"We can help," said Joe, but his heart sank when Hessa said, "Dasa, Joe. Let's start with clothes washing. That's an easy job. You can put all your dirty clothes in, too."

Francie was keen. She liked the feel and smell of clean clothes, and their clothes were truly filthy. But Joe hated laundry days: pumping and lugging buckets of water, sweating over a fire and then trying to wring water out of sodden clothes too heavy to lift. If washing was Hessa's idea of an easy job, he dreaded the hard ones.

He and Francie gathered the family's clothes and followed Hessa into a shed. There was no copper. Instead, Hessa put the clothes into a giant metal drum.

Joe looked underneath. "Where do you make the fire?"

"No need for fire." Hessa added some shaved soap and turned a tap in the wall. Hot water flowed in!

"Hot water?" Joe was astonished. "No carrying buckets? See that, Francie? No fire. Hot water straight from a tap. Let's live here forever!"

Francie did a little dance. She was as excited as Joe.

"How on earth does that work?"

"It's piped from the hot-water well. Hot along this pipe and cold along that one. I think everyone in Cruxcia has it. I thought everyone in the world would."

"Nowhere we've been," said Joe. "Now what do you do?"

Hessa clipped the drum shut and hung a weight on a chain that ran up to the ceiling through a series of pulleys, and down again to a spindle. The weight dropped slowly, turning the spindle, which turned the drum. Joe knew that wherever he lived in the future, he wanted water from a pipe, and a machine for washing clothes.

After a few minutes, Hessa opened the drain in the drum. When the dirty water had disappeared through a pipe in the floor she refilled the drum with cold water to rinse the clothes, then set it turning again to spin the water out.

As Joe watched the water flow into the drain, he thought about Beckett. Progress to him meant things like vulcanising machines and mining worms. Joe wondered if they had piped water and machines to wash clothes in New Coalhaven and Grand Prospect. He hadn't seen any and sensed that they didn't. Maybe Cruxcia was a better place. Hole-digging machines might be important to adults, but a system to bring water right into the wash house would make the most difference to children. Everywhere he'd ever been, children had the job of carrying home water. Water flowing through pipes right into every house, what an amazing idea!

"Hey, Francie, we should write to Beckett," he said. "He'd want to know about all this." Francie nodded. She perched on an old stool and began to draw: the clothes and the drum, the water pipes labelled *hot* and *cold*. They'd had a letter from Beckett before they left New Coalhaven telling them he'd got home safely and returned the donkeys to Mr Arbuckle, bought a milk cow, and had nearly finished mending the roof of his mother's house. He was still planning to buy a traction engine with the rest of his winnings.

Hessa looked at Francie's drawing. "How did you—? Did you just—? What the—?"

Francie smiled at her sketchbook.

"Amazing isn't it?" said Joe. "That's how we won the Great Race, because of Francie's drawings and maps."

Francie shook her head.

"It was *mostly* you," said Joe.

The tangle of clothes came out of the drum half-dry—no need

for wringing or a mangle! Hessa fed the hens and collected the eggs while Joe and Francie pegged them out on the clothesline. The Santanders' brown and grey clothes looked like a row of sparrows beside the parakeet colours of Terrabynd shirts and pants.

A pigeon flew into the pigeon house, and a bell rang to let them know. "I'll get the message," said Hessa, "then breakfast."

Chapter Seven

Land Grabbing

Sal had meant to help Hessa with the laundry too, but Vivi called her back. "Can I ask you something? I need your help."

"What to do?" Sal sat down beside her at the outdoor table.

"To save Cruxcia."

Sal nearly laughed, but Vivi wasn't joking. "In a few days, a judge is coming to register who owns what land in this valley. We need to prove that the land belongs to everyone in Cruxcia, and show that the farms have been cared for, often by the same family, for hundreds of years."

"But why?"

"Moustache Man and the GTC decreed that if you can't prove you own the land, they'll claim it for the GTC."

"They'll just take it? That's totally unfair!"

Vivi leaned back in her wheelchair. "It's stealing. And many of the valley people and townsfolk working on this claim have been arrested—including Tash. So now it's up to me." Vivi pushed a crusty loaf towards Sal. "It's bread and honey for breakfast."

Sal cut a slice. "How can I help?"

"The submission has to include an original, up-to-date map showing who cares for the land. We were worried about that part. But here you are! Three mapmakers. It seems the ancestors want us to keep going." Vivi passed Sal the honey. "If you can make a map of the valley, I'll put the names in."

"When d'you need it by?"

"The Land Court's in ten days. Two days after Hallowmas. Can you make a map that quickly? And in secret?"

Sal's insides tightened. "I need to think." She licked honey off her fingers. She wanted to help these people who were being so kind to them, but it depended on Francie. They'd won the Race because of Francie's flying, and her drawing skills. But the last time she'd flown was the day before the finish line on the Great Race, over three months ago now, when she'd flown for too long and nearly died. Could she still fly?

"I'll ask the others. But we came here to find our father, and now Ma and Humph are really sick—with worry about Pa probably, as well as from bad water. So, before we do anything, I need to go and check on Ma and tell her that Pa's alive."

"Of course," said Vivi.

"Can we visit Pa? Or at least get a message to him?"

"If only. All visitors are forbidden. No messages even." Vivi poured herself a mug of kafe and passed the pot.

Sal had never drunk kafe before. She poured herself half a cup. It didn't taste nearly as good as it smelled but she sipped at it anyway.

Hessa, Joe and Francie joined them at the table, all excited.

"Francie drew our wash house and she's better than a grown-up—she's as good an artist as Papa!" said Hessa.

"And Sal, you'll never guess what. They have hot water here that flows out of a pipe when you turn a lever!"

"We've done the hens, and the washing—" said Hessa.

"In a machine," said Joe.

Hessa gave Vivi a slip of paper. "A pigeon came in. Message from Lysander."

Vivi unrolled the paper and read aloud: *Something terrible happening on Mina Mendalwar—Cruxcia side. Urgent. Go and See.*

"On Mina Mendalwar? No! What next?" Hessa twirled round. "We've got to go. Right now. We can take breakfast with us."

While the others got organised, Sal ran to the shed. She whispered into the dark, "Hello Magnus, excuse me," and tiptoed past his perch. She dragged Ma's carpetbag into the square of light by the door and threw out Humph and Ma's sleeping bags, Ma's bag of lotions and potions, Humph's clothes and some papers. The bag was so heavy because of the golden guineas Ma had hidden, enough for the journey, plus a bit more.

Sal ran her fingers around the base of the empty bag, pressing each corner until she felt a click, then she lifted the bottom free. The gold coins gleamed. There had been five across, twelve along and five deep when they set off. Now, the coins were three deep, and two extra; one hundred and eighty-two coins. The rest were in the bank in New Coalhaven. Sal put the two loose coins into her new purse, then she shoved everything back in the bag and hid it under the sacks.

"Thanks, Magnus. Dasa."

Chapter Eight

Outrageous Desecration

"If you wear our clothes you'll be less noticeable." Vivi directed them to a cupboard in the living room where neatly folded shirts and pants were stacked on shelves. "The drawstrings mean they fit most people. And if any of the sandals in the shoe box fit, help yourselves."

Joe could feel how happy Francie was to change into loose cotton pants (red) and a baggy sky-blue shirt that she pulled over her head. He chose a green shirt and orange pants, and his feet were much cooler in sandals than they had been in boots. When Sal came back in, she changed as well.

Joe put a few sunflower seeds for Carrot on the table in the yard and told her to stay and make friend with the hens.

"Chook-chook, chooks?" She flew down among the hens, then screeched, "Worm eaters!" and flew into the tree.

Vivi disappeared into a shed and came out in a chair with several smaller-geared wheels inside looped tracks. She propelled it by pulling and pushing two levers, a bit like rowing.

"What an amazing vehicle," said Joe.

"Isn't she?" Vivi grinned. "I call her Doris."

They followed Vivi down the lane; Doris's tracks made easy work of the uneven ground, sailing over bumps and hollows. Other people were heading in the same direction, but Vivi was right about the Cruxcian clothing; no one even looked at them. Joe felt Francie's relief. Cruxcians came in all shapes, sizes and colours. Some even had orange hair, which Joe had never seen before. It was the Santanders' clothes that people had been staring at, not them.

Trees hung over the road, some still green, but others had turned red, yellow and brown, and some already had bare winter branches. Francie danced through the drifts of fallen leaves, and picked up special leaves to carry with her. Her delight in the autumn colours was catching, and lots of the people hurrying along anxiously paused to smile at her.

They walked on towards Mina Mendalwar, visible for miles around, like a great bun on the flat valley floor.

Ahead, they heard angry voices. A crowd stood watching on the river bank. On the far side, a row of tents had appeared since yesterday. Half a dozen men were busy on the grassy bank unrolling canvas and slotting poles together. Joe could hear an axe, and a tree above the campsite was quivering. There was a great crash as it smashed down through other trees.

Vivi shouted "No!" and Hessa clasped her forehead and murmured something that sounded a bit like praying, a bit like swearing.

Up and down the river bank people were yelling at the tent

men: *that's sacred land, you can't camp on our ancestors, leave our trees alone!* Someone threw a stone, but it plopped into the river. The men on the other side ignored the angry Cruxcians.

"I don't believe it. What are they doing? And why there?" Vivi said in a tight voice. She propelled herself closer for a clear view and started making notes.

"What about the fireworks?" Hessa's voice shook. "That's the best thing about Hallowmas, and they go off from right where they're putting the tents. I'm going to see what I can find out."

A team of eight oxen pulled a cart onto the green, followed by another and another.

Beside Joe, Vivi was scribbling fast. "Barrels, crates, sacks and machinery. But what's in all those barrels and crates? What sort of machinery?"

Joe looked through his telescope and suddenly the people seemed close enough to touch. "That man's carrying a pick-axe and a shovel. And I think that's an upside-down wheelbarrow—no, a stack of wheelbarrows—on the first cart, on top of a pile of wooden planks."

"It's outrageous desecration," Vivi muttered.

Outrageous desecration, Joe repeated in his head. Vivi had some really good words.

"There are eight big tents, so far. Each one could sleep at least six." Sal always counted everything. "And they're starting to pitch another one over there."

"So, this camp is for lots more people who haven't arrived yet." Vivi waved her arm. "And those vandals are attacking our trees."

Hessa arrived back panting. "It's a mining camp, people are

saying. Those men are miners. Moustache Man brought them here, but no one knows what for. I heard gold, coal and oil. We should go—Custodians just arrested someone who called Mundle something rude. Oh, and lots of people have said how sorry they are about Tash and to say if we need anything."

They followed Hessa away from the river.

"Everything has just got even more urgent." Vivi pushed one lever forward and pulled the other back, making Doris spin around on the spot. Her eyes were flashing. "I'm going to check some things in the archives."

"We'll go home then, shall we? And do some more of Tash's list?" said Hessa pointedly, but Vivi just waved and sped off.

Hessa spotted a friend in the crowd and ran to speak to her, which gave Sal a chance to make a huddle with Francie and Joe. "Vivi wants us to make a map, urgently, like the Cowboys are making. Can you go back to the house and try flying, Francie? Make sure you can do it and feel all right afterwards before I say yes to her?"

Francie nodded.

"I can keep an eye on you," said Joe, "and explain to Hessa. But where are you going, Sal?"

"To see Ma and Humphrey, and get Ma's purse. If there isn't much in it, I'll take a gold coin to the money-changer in the market and get us some Cruxcian money. With Tash in prison, too, we definitely need to help pay for food."

Hessa returned. "My friend Etta reckons that those men are after your mother because, she heard, there's a reward out for any Custodian who arrests a mapmaker."

Francie froze. Joe held her hand. "A reward—for us?"

"Not for you. No one knows you're mapmakers too, do they?"

Sal shook her head. "The Cowboys know, but they don't know we're here. Unless—do Tall and Short know, Joe?"

"They nearly found out," said Joe. "Thank goodness we didn't let them see your sketchbook, Francie."

As they waved goodbye to Sal, Joe felt guilty but glad that she was the one going to the infirmary. It had been so frightening seeing Ma and Humphrey so ill, he didn't want to see them again until he knew they were getting better. And Sal would get Cruxcian money—he'd never have thought of that, but she was right, they should pay for things. She always did the worrying, but maybe that was how she managed to think of things like needing money. He was glad he wasn't the eldest.

Chapter Nine

The Chase

Sal's Cruxcian pants had deep pockets closed with a button, so her new purse was safe. Cruxcian clothes were so sensible.

She found her way to the apothecary and alchemy part of town, checking often that no one was following. All the shopfronts looked similar, so she asked two girls playing hopscotch if they knew where Pi lived. They led her around the corner and pointed out the entrance. Sal was embarrassed not to have a coin for them, but they laughed and hopped back to their game.

Auntie Pi opened the door and greeted her the Cruxcian way. "Come in, Sal. I heard about Tash. Are the girls managing all right?"

"They're fine. They seem really good at managing," said Sal.

"They're experts. Go through. Humphrey's recovering fast. Your mother's still quite poorly. I'm making arrangements to move them somewhere the Custodians won't think to look."

"Thank you."

Humph and Ma were still side by side in their low bed. Humph's cheeks were now scarlet, but Ma was pale as pale.

"Hello, Ma and Humphrey."

Humph sat up, pleased to see her. "Sal, my Sal! I just ate tostas."

"That's good."

"And my eyes have stopped crying."

"Excellent! It sounds like you're getting better." Sal sat on the bed and gave him a cuddle. Auntie Pi passed her a drink and she held the cup until he'd swallowed it all. Afterwards he seemed happy enough to lie down again and suck his thumb.

Sal crouched at Ma's side of the bed and took her hand; it was hot and dry. Her eyes were shut. "Ma? Ma? Are you asleep? It's me, Sal." Ma groaned quietly. Sal squeezed her fingers and whispered, "I've got good news to make you feel better. Pa's alive! He's in prison, like a lot of people here. But he's alive!"

Sal had so wanted to be the one to give Ma the wonderful news. She'd imagined Ma reacting with joy—throwing her arms around her and even making an instant recovery. But Ma showed no sign of having heard. Sal tried to sing "The Wind Blows Softly", which Ma sang to her when she was little, but the lump in her throat was too big. She held Ma's hand for a while, and Humphrey fell asleep.

Ma's rucksack was hanging from a hook on the wall. Sal fished out Ma's purse. Too light, just three tiny coins. She'd have to brave the money-changer.

"I've got some jobs to do. I'll be back soon, Humpty."

"We have a couple of Tash's pigeons up in the loft. We'll

let you know when we move your mother and how she and Humphrey are doing." Pi had an abrupt way of speaking but her smile was kind. "I'm glad you're with the girls."

Vivi had told Sal of a money-exchange kiosk near the market entrance. The man behind the counter looked curiously at her golden sovereign. He weighed it and scraped it with the point of a knife. He seemed satisfied that it really was gold and counted out a pile of Cruxcian coins. Then he looked up and noticed someone. He called out. Sal turned. Two men were striding towards the kiosk: Lieutenant Loofus and Private Clocksley. "That's the Santander girl. Stop her, Clocksley!"

The money-changer still had her sovereign in his fist. What could she do? She snatched up the local money in both hands and ran with it, a few coins clattering on the cobblestones behind her. Loofus shouted at her to stop, but there was no way she would she let them catch another Santander.

The crowd made way for her, opening gaps as she ran. Before she got far, though, she skidded on wet cabbage leaves and fell, skinning her knuckles and cracking her knee on a stone, but not dropping a single coin. Ow-ow-ow-ow-ow. Her knee hurt a lot, but she scrambled up and kept running.

The Custodians were still following. Which way to go? She turned onto the main thoroughfare. Now where? Up the hill. At the next crossroads, she turned left and then right and sprinted over the road in front of a laden wagon, horribly close to the carthorse's great hooves, and whatever the driver shouted at her didn't sound polite. She called "Sorry" as she slipped round the next corner.

Were they still coming? She looked in a shop window to see the reflection of the street behind her. There was a flash of maroon and gold as the Custodians turned the corner and came on, fast. Ahead, two more Custodians were coming towards her. They hadn't spotted her yet but as soon as they did, she'd be trapped.

Then she heard a male voice call, "Here! Quick!" from somewhere above her. An elderly woman held a shop door open and jerked her head at Sal. "He's through there."

The woman gestured her through an inner door and shut it

behind her. Sal was in a dark room packed with flowers hanging in bunches from the ceiling, like an upside-down garden. The scent made her giddy.

The voice called again, "Over here, quick." Sal ducked and felt her way in the gloom. Then she was in a passage, moving towards the voice. It led her to a steep staircase. She followed a pair of large sandaled feet as they climbed up and up, around and around. Thirty-one, thirty-two, thirty-three. Her knee was really throbbing. Sixty-five, sixty-six, sixty-seven. Where were they going? And was she crazy to follow this stranger?

The final flight was more ladder than stairs. She had to use her hands that were still clutching the money, so she slid all the coins into her pockets. At ninety-nine she stepped off the ladder at the top of the building. She was in a square room with glassless windows on all four sides and a blissfully cool breeze blowing through—and the soft murmurings of many pigeons cooing from their perches. In the middle of the room was a large circular cage, the floor of which was covered in bird poo, feathers and spilt bird seed.

She was relieved to see that the feet belonged to a smiling boy not much older than her, wearing a long green shirt and pink trousers, and a scarf tied pirate-style around his head. As soon as she was off the ladder, he hauled on a rope and it rose into the room. He flipped a trapdoor down over the hole and grinned. "I've always wanted an excuse to do that." He held a finger up to his mouth. "Shhh—they're checking the house now."

Sal stood, tense, and listened to clumping boots, huffing and puffing, and quite a bit of swearing. It got louder and louder, then gradually quieter as the Custodians went back down the stairs. Her knees felt wobbly with relief. She sank down onto a window seat.

"They'll search the lower floors, then they'll have to listen to Grandma Clarrie lecturing them about scaring old people. When we hear her whistle, I'll show you how to get back to Vivi and Hessa's."

"Oh, you know them!" Her relief was followed by a realisation. "Wait, you're Lysander—the pigeons—messages. I'm Sal."

He touched his fingers to his forehead. "I am Lysander Klim, son of Kerala and Kester, citizen of Cruxcia. Vivi and Hessa are my cousins. Pi and Tash are my mother's sisters."

Sal touched her own forehead. It was feeling more natural now. "How did you know I needed help?"

"I was watching the street." He shook bird seed into a feeder. "Did you go and see the camp?"

"We did. Vivi and Hessa are upset."

"We all are." He nodded at Sal's knee. "You're hurt."

Sal looked. Blood was seeping through so she rolled up her trouser leg. The graze was messy. She felt for a handkerchief—why didn't she ever have a hankie when she needed one? Lysander passed her his, and she pressed it against the wound. "I've just been to Pi's. She's looking after my mother and brother. They're sick."

"I heard," said Lysander. "And now, Hessa and Vivi's parents are both in prison, as are mine."

"Yours are too? How awful! What did they do?"

"They *do*? They were accused of 'Civil Disobedience in the

second degree'—they were trying to stop the Cowboy mapmakers. There wasn't a trial."

"Are they alright? My father's in prison too."

"I know." This boy knew everything—or thought he did. It was annoying. "I think they're 'alright'. Alive. But sad."

"I don't know if our father had a trial. We thought he was dead." Sal's eyes tingled. "And now our mother is really sick, so is our little brother and I'm just—" she sniffed. "I'm really tired. Sorry. The Custodians are chasing me because they want to arrest Ma. And those Cowboys that your parents tried to stop are really dangerous. They even kidnapped my little brother—it's all right, he escaped—but, but, it's all too much. Everyone here's so kind, but…"

To Sal's horror, she burst into tears. There was nothing to be done, so she wrapped her arms around her shins, head to knees, and sobbed until she was all dried out and hiccup-y. She blew her nose on Lysander's handkerchief, which was bloodied from her knee.

Lysander passed her a flask. "It's good well water."

She drank gratefully and blew her nose again hard then stood up. "I need to get back, they'll be worried."

"We'll send a message." Lysander snatched up a sharp pencil and a pad of very thin paper.

Sal wrote: *I am safe. Met Lysander. Back soon. Sal*

Lysander folded the paper in half, rolled it up and slid it into a tiny metal cylinder. He reached into the cage and lifted out a bird. He tucked it under his arm and clipped the cylinder to a band on its leg, then took the pigeon to the window and tossed it out. For one horrible moment Sal thought it was going to plummet to the ground, but it soared upwards and disappeared.

"How does it know where to go?"

"They're homing pigeons. The ones in this half of the cage are the Terrabynds', so that's where they go. The birds on the other side live here."

He poked the spout of a watering can through the bars and filled a trough.

"So the crate of pigeons yesterday was yours? From here?" said Sal. "That's very clever."

"They're actually my mother's. So she can message her sisters. I'm just looking after them."

Three sharp toots whistled from below, followed by a long blast.

"That's Grandma. The Custodians have gone." Lysander lifted the hatch and lowered the ladder. At the bottom of the stairs he called, "Back later," to his grandmother, then led the way through a storeroom full of vats and barrels and out onto a street on the other side of the building.

Lysander checked up and down. "All clear." He walked fast, with long strides. Mostly Sal didn't care that she'd stopped growing upwards and that Joe and Francie were now as tall as her, but she felt awkward that she was sweating and panting trying to keep up with Lysander. And her knee hurt.

"Lysander?" She hurried after him. "What sort of things do people do against the Cowboys? What is civil disobedience?"

Lysander side-stepped for a boy with a handcart piled with crates. "All sorts of things. My parents went round swapping the arms of signposts so the Cowboys rode off in the wrong direction. One night they even helped build a two-metre-high dry-stone wall right across the road."

"Clever! And it explains what we heard the Cowboys talking about." She told Lysander how frightening it was to see Cody Cole in the restaurant, and how they'd heard him boast that they'd caught the last of the trouble-makers.

"There's no 'last' of trouble-makers. We all make trouble. Some days, the Cowboy horses can't move because someone's opened a gate and the road is full of sheep. Or geese chase them. Or a cart's lost its wheel and is blocking a narrow lane. It's very funny."

"Not so funny to be in prison though," said Sal. She felt cheered by the thought of so many people making life difficult for the Cowboys. She was almost hopeful, an unfamiliar feeling. Joe usually did enough hoping for both of them; she had to be the worrier to balance him out.

They walked in silence for a while, out of town and on to the river road. Lysander not only walked fast, he sometimes spun round and jiggled as if he were dancing to a secret tune in his head. Sal asked about the upside-down flowers.

"They're for the soap my mother makes. Soap for people, for clothes, for machines, even for saddles. She makes it, and Grandma Clarrie runs the shop."

He lived above the shop with his parents and grandmother. He had older sisters with their own houses and children.

Sal couldn't tell how old Lysander was. "Do you go to school?"

"No, thank goodness. My father, Kester, is a pyrotechnician. I'm apprenticed to him."

"What's a pyro-thingy?"

"Fireworks. I'm learning to make fireworks."

Sal was astonished. "Isn't that incredibly dangerous?"

"It can be." Lysander showed her a recent scar across his palm. Then he stopped and pointed at the nearest of two low buildings standing alone between the road and the river. "That's our pyrotechnic workshop. The other one's the Terrabynd paint studio. Can you find your way from here?"

"Straight on, then left at the field with the haystack."

"Good to meet you." He touched his forehead. "I'll see you again soon. Voh'mah berrin. Luck be with you."

The roof of the house was the perfect place to fly from: private, comfy and quiet. Joe helped Francie make a nest with the sleeping bags and fetched water and honey for afterwards. Then he sat on the top step and waited while she flew.

Up and up. Above Joe eating honey, above Vivi and Hessa's roof, above chickens. Higher. Everything is ringed with light and shimmering. Trees are fire-coloured—crimson, scarlet, umber, sienna, gold—and the water in the river ripples and dances. The beautiful, beautiful world.

The river curves between Mina Mendalwar and Cruxcia; there's the miners' campsite. There's banging and clanging and shouting below. The trees are trembling in fear and the air shivers.

Miners stand in the leaves of the tree they felled. They are splitting the trunk, piling up green firewood, surrounded by trees and headstones.

Away from Mina Mendalwar, on past the market, and the Sky Worff—one dirigible, three ornithopters. The river is shallower. Not a single band now but many threads, criss-crossing, weaving together and separating. Beyond, the riverbed is etched on the land, dry as a dusty stone road waiting for rain.

There is other life on the plain. Down, closer. Tents, children playing, families, camels, donkeys, goats, patches of garden. Nomads?

Up again, round. Three ancient ways come together at Cruxcia market. Laden camels sway towards the town along the track from the south. A second track comes from over the mountains and follows the River Afa to Cruxcia. The third comes from the north-west, following the curves of the land where the mountains meet the plain. People and animals are travelling along it. Before it gets to the market it passes close to buildings inside a giant wall. Closer. The prison! Pa, Pa, are you there?

Over the top then around the prison again. Watchtowers at each corner. No prisoners to be seen outside.

Back along the river. To the kaleidoscope house.

Tired. Back to body.

Chapter Ten

The Prison

When Joe saw Francie sitting up, he laughed with relief. He'd been fairly sure she'd be able to fly again, but what if she hadn't? He gave her a spoonful of honey, and she sucked it eagerly. Then her hand raced over her sketchbook. She drew the town and Mina Mendalwar and the river disappearing away over the plain.

Joe's twin was a triple genius: not only could she fly and see the world from above, she could remember anything she saw, and she could draw it perfectly. It was just a quick sketch map—her paper was too small for much detail, but she added an unexpected feature. She drew a man. Pa!

"The prison. You saw it? Did you see Pa?"

She hunched over and shook her head. No prisoners, just the prison. He could tell that she'd been affected by seeing it, but he didn't know what else to ask. He hugged her. Some things were too hard to draw, even for Francie.

Joe checked that Francie was happy for him to tell Hessa

about flying, before she sucked another spoonful of honey and climbed into the hammock under the awning. She needed to sleep after flying.

Hessa was picking low-growing beans and piling them into the laundry basket. Joe joined in the picking while he explained about Francie's special powers. How her body would stay where she lay, while she rose up and viewed the land as if she were a bird. And that was how she could draw perfect maps.

"Flying." Hessa didn't seem surprised. "How lucky! I want to fly more than anything. What a wonderful power for a mapmaker."

"Ma thinks her great-aunt could fly, and her great-grandfather, so it's in the family. They couldn't draw as well as Francie, though. She only needs to see something once to draw it perfectly."

"Like Vivi. She only has to read something once and she can remember it all, and bore you with it for hours. I'm just ordinary." Hessa started pulling out the old bean plants.

"Sal's a maths genius. And she's sometimes a bit—" How to explain Sal? "too full of thoughts to know what's going on. But I'm just ordinary, too. We could start an Ordinary People's Club." Joe piled the old plants together. "Where do these go?"

"Just leave them in a heap for now. Perhaps you have special skills but you don't recognise them."

"Like what?" They carried the laundry basket between them to the table.

"Well, you know how some people are really kind and everyone likes them? Maybe that's a special skill."

Joe's throat tightened. "Pa's like that."

Two pigeons arrived. Hessa picked up a bird and showed Joe how to hold it to take off the message. It was from Sal. She'd met Lysander and was on her way home. The other pigeon had a message from Auntie Pi, who said that Custodians were nosing around so she was moving Ma and Humphrey to a safe place. She asked them not to visit for now, in case they were followed, but promised to send regular pigeon updates.

Joe felt a bit mixed up. "Good that she's safe, but I wanted to see her."

"Maybe send a message instead." Hessa showed him where the message paper and tubes lived.

He sucked the end of his pencil. What should he say? There was only room for a few words, and the fewer words he wrote the more special he felt they should be. In the end he just sent love and xxxx, and Francie woke up in time to decorate the corners of the paper with tiny birds. She rolled the paper into the tube and Hessa clipped it to the leg of one of Auntie Pi's pigeons and gave it to Francie to release. It flew up and up, then turned and headed for the town.

When Sal got back, Joe told her that Francie had seen the prison.

"Oh, Francie. Is it scary? Is it horrible?"

Francie nodded.

Sal hugged her, and explained what Vivi needed them to do. "We're going to map the valley for the Cruxcian land claim, and while we're mapping we've got to look out for other clues about what the GTC and Mundle are up to."

Joe knew without looking that Francie was feeling more cheerful. "Mapping," he said, "is exactly the thing we feel like doing."

Hessa fetched some of her special homemade ginger beer and they sat on the roof while Sal told them about being chased by the Custodians and meeting Lysander, and the very tall house and the pigeons. Hessa asked about the blood on Sal's trousers. Joe fetched the lotions and potions bag and found Ma's magic cream for Sal's knee.

"Lysander said his parents have both been arrested, too," said Sal.

Hessa nodded. "It's true. But if you promise not to breathe a word to anyone, I'll tell you a secret." They promised, and Hessa lowered her voice. "Vivi and some friends—*not* the Town Council—are making a plan to get all the prisoners out."

Sal leaned forward. "A real escape plan?"

Francie grabbed Sal's hand and squeezed hard.

"It has to stay completely secret," said Hessa. "If the GTC or any of Moustache Man's spies find out, they'll bring in a whole lot more warders and probably surround the prison with Custodians and cannons."

"We won't breathe a word. Oh, if only!" Sal crossed her legs, and her arms and her fingers. "Can we help?"

"What are they going to do?" asked Joe.

"Don't know yet." Hessa swung in the hammock. "But Vivi's the best plan-maker in the world."

Joe could believe that. He tried to picture Pa. A year was a long time, though, and the picture was fuzzy. What if he didn't recognise Pa? And Joe had grown a lot—what if Pa didn't recognise him, either? The thought that they could pass each other on the street and never know made his heart hurt.

Then Vivi rolled through the gate. She was red-faced, panting, and her shirt had damp patches.

"Vivi!" Hessa ran down the stairs. "What happened? Are you all right?"

"Drink!" she gasped.

Hessa poured her a mug of water and she drank it straight down. Hessa refilled the mug with ginger beer and that went straight down too.

"News." Vivi's voice was still dry and raspy. "They're going to move the prisoners. In eight days! After that it'll be too late to free them—they'll be gone."

Chapter Eleven

Spying

"Where are they taking them?"

"Why?"

"How do you know?"

They bombarded Vivi with questions.

"I am so angry I'm going to burst. Pass me some windfalls, Hessa," said Vivi.

Hessa nodded. She put a basket full of bruised and wormy apples on Vivi's lap, then set up a row of flowerpots on the orchard wall. Vivi picked out an apple. "The GTC are money-grubbing slugs." She hurled it, and the first pot fell. "Mundle should be chopped into little pieces and fed to the crocodiles." An apple hit the second pot. She paused. "If I get the next one, it means Tash and Taliesin will escape." Wham, her apple knocked the third pot to the edge of the wall. Where it teetered … then fell into the long grass of the orchard.

"Hooray!" said Hessa. "Three out of three."

"That's enough. My arms are dead," said Vivi.

"Start again, please," said Sal. "Explain everything."

"The GTC are moving the prisoners to another prison on Hallowmas Day. Eight days away. The day after Lysander's fireworks and the day before the Land Court hearing."

"Then we'll have to get them out before Hallowmas," said Sal.

"Exactly," said Vivi.

"How did you find out?" asked Hessa.

"You know I went to the archives?" Vivi looked at her hands. They were trembling. "Have we anything to eat?"

Hessa reached for the sunderstrum tin.

"Thanks. Well, that was a waste of time. Mundle's had all the records relating to land in the valley taken to the Mundle mansion—cartloads of them. I talked to the apprentice archivist and she was fuming about it—and not just because she'd hurt her back lugging them all.

"While we were talking, this dirigible pilot came in. Her boyfriend. When they started kissing, I rolled out of sight, but I could still hear them talking. Turns out he'd promised to take her family up in a dirigible for a treat on Hallowmas Day. He'd come to say sorry, he's been told he has to work instead, and all the dirigibles have been booked for the whole day. She asked why, and he said—"

"The GTC, to move the prisoners," said Hessa and Joe together.

"Exactly," said Vivi.

"Ten out of ten, well done," said Carrot, landing on the table.

"Thanks, Carrot," said Hessa.

"The pilot went on to say, 'It's totally top secret, you won't say anything will you?' and she said, 'No, of course not'. It's not just prisoners going, it's warders and lots of Custodians too. He said he was lucky because all he had to do was fly them wherever and come back. But lots of warders and Custodians are unhappy because they'll have to stay there."

"So we need a plan to free the prisoners, urgent, urgent, urgent," said Sal.

"We're so close. We're not losing Pa again," said Joe.

"Hear hear," said Carrot.

Francie stroked her cheek against the parrot's soft back.

"There there," said Carrot. "Hear, there."

Vivi poured herself another mug of ginger beer. "I thought of waiting until the prisoners were being taken to the Sky Worff, but they'll likely be chained together; also, the Custodians have guns. We have to get them out of the actual prison. Through a gate or over the wall." Vivi looked in the sunderstrum tin but it was empty. "When I was in the archives, I looked for the records of the prison. Maps. Plans. Designs. Materials ordered—but there's nothing. It's like it doesn't exist."

Francie nudged Sal and jerked her head at Vivi. Of course!

"If you need one, we can make a plan of the prison, easy," Sal said. "Or rather, Francie can."

"How?" said Vivi. "There's nowhere you can see it all from, is there? Unless you steal an ornithopter."

They told Vivi about Francie's flying, and Francie opened her sketchbook to the morning's map of the whole area, and the drawing she'd done with Pa walking free.

Vivi looked, and looked closer, then she and Hessa laughed

and hugged. "This is astonishing. Extraordinary. Thank you. A map of the prison would make all the difference in the world." She bit her lip. "Time's short, though. Eight days to get them out, ten days until the Land Court. We can do it … can't we?"

She didn't sound so sure. Francie started rocking gently in her seat. Joe put an arm round her.

"We can do it," said Sal.

"We don't just need a map of the prison," said Hessa. "We need to know what the different buildings are for. And when the warders change shifts, and go to bed and that sort of thing. I think we should go and spy on it—I know a place where you can see most of the buildings from. Let's go now; Francie can draw and we can spy on the prison all night."

While Hessa organised a bag of snacks and water flasks, Joe fetched their sleeping bags. Stracky arrived with an apple cake and pasties from his mother.

"This looks like a silver lining," said Vivi, and Hessa added four pasties and half the cake to her picnic basket.

Joe suggested they change into dark clothes. There was nothing black to wear in the kaleidoscope house, so they settled for brown and dark blue.

Vivi checked that Sal had plenty of blank pages in her notebook. "The more we know the better. Do Custodians work at the prison, or is it just warders? Do they patrol the grounds at night? What are all the buildings for; where do the prisoners sleep? It's supposed to be a clear night and there'll be a bit of moon for writing. This could be so good!" She sounded excited and a bit wistful.

Sal nodded. "I'll write everything down."

"Do you have a pocket watch we could take?" asked Joe. "So we can make a note of *when* things happen."

Hessa ran to their parents' bedroom and emerged with a silver watch on a chain. "It's our papa's. It's luminous, you can read it in the dark."

Sal passed the precious watch to Francie. Francie never lost anything, and only ever broke things if she meant to.

"Please bolt the gate, and the door, and don't open them for anyone," said Hessa.

"I promise," said Vivi and hugged her. She looked at the Santanders. "Are you sure you'll be all right sitting out on a hillside in the dark?"

"We'll be fine," said Sal. "We've come a long way to find Pa; we want him back. Only eight days to go."

They walked in a line along the narrow footpath above the town, then down through an olive grove, under some scratchy bushes and out onto a ridge with a view over the plain.

The plain was dotted with clumps of trees and stretched all the way to a smudge of mountains on the horizon. Below them, the main route north-west hugged the bottom of the hill, and a hundred metres away, an access lane led off the road to an imposing gatehouse in the high wall that enclosed the prison.

The prison. Sal's eyes blurred with tears. She blinked and swallowed hard. Somewhere inside that wall was Pa.

They passed the telescope between them. Joe focused on the wall. "It's unclimbable. Smooth as Francie's drawing pad."

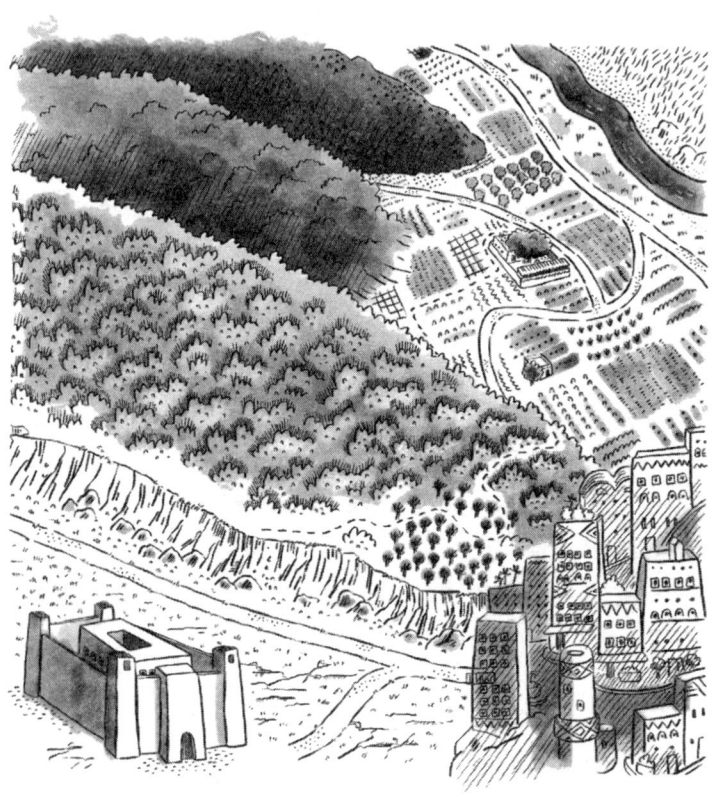

It was Sal who noticed a high fence running along inside the wall. "It's not just the wall we have to get over; there's a double barrier. And the gap is guarded by dogs."

Everything they saw was cause for despair.

"There are women coming out!" Hessa squeaked. "Walking in a line. Let me look—maybe I can see Tash." She took the telescope. "They're all wearing yellow. That's Auntie Kerala, Lysander's mother." Hessa started to wave, then lowered the telescope and wiped her face on her sleeve. "She seemed so close."

Hessa looked again. "There are lots of them walking round and round. There's Lilja's mother, and Madoc and Etta's mother. And Tash!" She stood up and hit her head on a branch. "Ow." She rubbed her eyes. "She looks worried. I wish she could see me. They're being watched by brown uniforms. Must be the warders."

Francie nodded.

The women did two more circuits of the long building then went inside. Sal hoped that the male prisoners would come out next, but no one else appeared. Francie snuggled down in her sleeping bag and made herself comfortable.

"Sure you feel up to flying again, Francie?" asked Sal.

Francie smiled.

Up and up. Joe, Sal, Hessa tucked under bushes, hiding. Joe's telescope to his eye, Sal writing, writing.

Over the road, over the prison wall. Buildings make patterns and shadows. See the shapes, know the shapes. In each corner a watchtower.

Are you here, Pa?

Below south-west tower—strings of brown bunting. Closer. Washing lines hold brown uniforms swaying to the air music. Warder unpegging, folding. Takes full basket into building behind.

Around the back, a yard. Prisoners carry firewood from stack. Not Pa. Armload, armload. Warders waving truncheons. Hurry, hurry, hurry. Yellow person drops log, bends to pick it up. Warder kicks. Prisoner sprawls.

Bad feelings, bad feelings.

Beyond, near north-west corner, a pigeon house. A pigeon brings in message.

In the open, one, two, three, four little round huts. Closer. Warders watching, watching.

Once more around. Pa? Where are you, Pa?

Warder with big hat leads no-hat warders to small flat-roofed building. Big hat bends with keys. Door opens. Big hat brings out rifles.

No-no-no.

Spinning, spinning.

Look. Must look. One gun each. Target near fence. Take turns. Shoot, shoot, shoot. Each time a little puff of air. Dogs race up and down behind fence.

Once more around. No yellow prisoners. No Pa.

Chapter Twelve

Amazement

Joe had Francie's drawing board pinned with fresh paper, all ready for her when she sat up. Without looking at him, she picked up a pencil. Five minutes later she'd drawn not only a perfect plan of the prison, but also a series of pictures showing what happened where: the laundry, the pigeon loft, the place where supplies arrived and were unloaded, the cookhouse, the courtyard in the middle of the warders' lodge, the four little lookouts, the dog-runs, the rifle range, the armoury and the dormitories.

When she'd finished, she sucked a spoonful of honey and lay down to sleep.

Hessa stared. "I have amazement spilling out of my ears."

"Just like I told you," said Joe. "Triple genius."

"There's smoke coming from those chimneys," said Sal. "They must be making dinner."

"I'm hungry, too," said Hessa. "Pastie time."

They ate pasties and apples and nuts Hessa had brought that were really hard to get out of their shell.

"It must be very boring in prison," said Hessa. "It's boring just watching a prison."

Not for long. A bell rang. Two trolleys with pots on them were trundled out of the chimney building—the cookhouse—and one was wheeled into each of the long dormitory buildings. Prisoners' dinners.

Lamps were lit. At half-past six they watched the night warders take over from the day warders, who all went into the building next to the cookhouse. Warders' dining room, they decided. Lamplight shone through the windows of the warders' lodge.

On the hillside it was completely dark.

"Did you see that?" asked Sal. "Three lanterns left each of the watchtowers, but no lanterns have gone back in. Does that mean no warders in the watchtowers?"

They kept spying as long as they could, but nothing much happened and they dozed off until the first light of a cold dawn.

Joe checked through his telescope as soon as he could see the prison. "I spy three warders going to each watchtower. And none leaving."

They set off back to the kaleidoscope house after they'd seen the prisoners' breakfasts delivered. "I hope there's been a message from Auntie Pi," said Sal.

"And I want to get under some hot rain," said Hessa.

"What's hot rain?" asked Joe.

"Really? You don't know? You wait, it's the best thing ever!" Hessa threw open the door to the house.

Vivi looked up from her papers.

"We've mapped it!" Hessa cried. "It's brilliant. Francie is amazing. We've been awake practically all night and it was quite boring. But guess what? The Santanders have never had hot rain, so hot rain first, then kafe and tostas. You won't believe what Francie can do. Have a look at this."

They left Vivi with the map, drawings and notes and followed Hessa to a small room where the floor, walls and ceiling were covered with tiles in every imaginable colour. Towels hung from pegs on the door. Francie stroked the wall. Hessa pushed a lever and hot rain showered down from above. Steam billowed.

"Now I'm the one with amazement coming out of me," said Joe.

"Girls first." Hessa shooed him out and shut the door.

A bell pinged as a pigeon flew into the pigeon house. Joe went to investigate. The bird had landed on a bar that had triggered the bell. Joe lifted the pigeon out, cradling its warm body as Hessa had shown him; its heart was racing under his fingers. It carrooooed to the other pigeons perched around the loft as he tucked it under his armpit and unclipped the message tube. The girls were still in the hot rain shed, so he took it inside to Vivi.

She looked up from the map of the prison and the notes and pictures. Her eyes were shining. "I really think Francie's been sent by the ancestors. With all this information, we may actually be able to free the prisoners!"

"I thought we could steal a dirigible," said Joe, "hover over the prison and let down a rope ladder, but actually, climbing a rope ladder's really hard and takes too long. My best idea is to dig a tunnel under the wall and the fence. A message came." He passed her the tube.

Vivi unrolled the flimsy bit of paper. "Auntie Pi says Humphrey's better. Full of bounce. I think that means she wants to get rid of him. Lysander's bringing him here later. Your mother's better, too, sitting up and keeping fluids down. She ends with *send pigeons*."

Joe ran out into the bright sunshine and banged on the door of the hot rain room. "Ma's getting better! She's awake and drinking."

There were cheers and shouts through the door.

Humphrey was coming. Good. He wouldn't be so outnumbered by girls. He went back inside and asked Vivi, "What did it mean 'send pigeons'?"

"She needs more of ours, to send more messages. Stracky will take some over this afternoon. And bring back some of hers, because we've run out."

Chapter Thirteen

The Wisps of a Plan—and Scrolls

Sal could have stayed under the hot rain all day, but they turned it off eventually to let Joe have a go. She'd never felt so clean. Her hair and skin smelled of Lysander's mother's soap and they had clean clothes after yesterday's laundering.

Joe, Francie and Hessa went up to the roof after breakfast and fell asleep in the sun, but Sal was wide awake. She was ready to make a plan. Vivi was outside making more kafe. "You'll need kafe if you're not having a nap," she said.

"We have seven days left." Sal poured herself a small cup.

"Yes, we need a plan. Once we've worked out the escape, I can organise what we need while you're busy mapping the valley."

That sounded reasonable. Sal knew she wouldn't be much help finding a locksmith or a fence cutter—but she could make a map.

They bent over Francie's drawings and Vivi asked questions. "The doors marked B are just bolted from the outside?"

"That's what Francie saw."

"And the gun store?"

"She drew that keyhole and two padlocks, so it's well locked."

"And there are no warders in the watchtowers at night?"

"Only until half past six in the evening. After that they use those four round lookouts. They swap round every few hours between the gatehouse and the lookouts and this building we called the office."

"How many warders in each lookout?"

"It's hard to be sure. But the lookouts are really small. There was only one person in each during the day."

"And the carts get checked going in and out?"

"They even looked under the horses' girths," said Sal.

"So, we can't go in—or out—hanging under horses." Vivi grinned. "Bang goes my entire plan!" She flicked her pen through her fingers. "That leaves cunning trickery or sheer force of numbers. If everyone in the whole town just barged into the prison together…"

"The Custodians would shoot them before they got there, and the gates are all locked," said Sal.

"True. Ladders at night?" said Vivi.

"You'd need a lot of time or a lot of ladders. And don't forget the dogs."

"I wonder if Nomie could help with the dogs?"

"Who's Nomie?"

"Aunti Pi's partner. She's an apothecary too, but for animals. Hey, what about a wooden horse with rescuers inside it, like the Greeks used against the Trojans?"

"Then you'd have even more people to get out." Sal considered. "I like the idea of involving everyone in the town."

"Me too, but we must be careful with our plans. A few—a very few—of them are spies for the GTC and Mundle."

"If any of the Custodians and warders don't want to go to the new prison, they might be persuaded to change sides," said Sal.

"Good thinking! And Stracky said he's had an idea about access to the prison. We have the wisps of a plan."

It was midday before Hessa, Joe and Francie woke up.

Hessa was upset. "It's nearly Hallowmas. It's supposed to be family time—we haven't even got the trees out."

"Oh, we should," said Vivi.

"I'll fetch them." Hessa ran into the house and brought out two scrolls. "These are our family trees. They're supposed to come out of the box a week before Hallowmas. We hang them up to remember our ancestors and tell stories about them. That's Taliesin's tree and this is Tash's."

Joe helped her unroll Tash's tree on the table. The branches were dotted with names and dates of birth and death.

"This woman was a great mathematician, unlike any of us. This one was a town commissioner and a very good arguer, like me." Vivi pointed to names. "In this man's portrait, he's got the exact same curly hair as Hessa. And that one is supposed to have lain under a tree for a whole year thinking about leaves."

Why anyone would do such a thing, Sal couldn't imagine. But how extraordinary to know about all your ancestors. She'd heard only a few stories involving their grandparents, great-aunts and great-uncles. The only relatives she knew were a sister, two brothers, a sick mother and a father she hadn't seen for nearly a year. "I wish we could tell Pa we're here in Cruxcia," she said.

Francie looked up from her drawing pad and nodded. She'd been thinking the same.

There was a knock on the gate. Hessa opened it and returned with a heavy pot. "Dinner from Idris's mother."

"And I was about to say that I wished someone else would make dinner," said Vivi. "Magic powers!"

They all laughed.

"Let's have it for linner," said Hessa.

"Linner?" asked Joe.

"A big meal about four o'clock," said Hessa. "Until then, I'll do some garden work. I still haven't found Tash's list but I know most of it."

"We'll help," said Sal.

They left Vivi with her papers and took baskets into the vegetable garden. Hessa showed Sal how to pick the courgettes and she came along behind her, pulling up the plants that had finished producing. They had big leaves and they came out of the ground easily. Joe pulled up the finished purple-bean plants and dismantled the frame. Francie put on gloves and picked peppers and chillies.

"Good teamwork," said Hessa. "This would have taken me hours on my own."

They were washing their hands at the tap when the gate flew open and Humphrey cannon-balled across the courtyard.

"I'm here!" he shouted, and threw himself at Sal. "I'm all better and I came with Pirate Dander."

Carrot shrieked. "One, three, four, two. All here."

Those who didn't know each other were introduced, except for Francie who moved behind the tree and watched from there. Lysander greeted them, fingers to forehead, and Humphrey copied him.

"Are you all better?" Sal asked Humphrey. "You don't feel sick any more?"

"He's better," said Lysander. "We had to run races most of the way here."

"Pirate Dander is a pirate," Humphrey said to Sal in a loud whisper.

Sal laughed. "No he's not, he's a pyrotechnician. It's quite different."

"Why's he wear a pirate hat then? Because he's a pirate, silly!"

The gate opened again and Stracky heaved a basket of pigeons into the yard. "Shala! I'll take yours back if they're ready."

Sal helped Hessa carry the basket into the pigeon house. They unclipped the lid and the newly arrived pigeons jostled into the empty side of the loft. They refilled the basket with ten Terrabynd pigeons and carried it out to the cart, wedging it between a sack of potatoes and a crate of cauliflowers so it wouldn't slide about.

"Now let's send a message to Ma," said Sal.

Hessa fetched a pad of tissue-thin paper and Francie took a pencil from her hair. She drew a tiny pigeon flying between two even tinier houses.

Sal wrote: *We are all well and here together.* "I don't want to say that Tash has been arrested because she'll worry. What else can I say?"

"Say we're happy," suggested Joe.

"Say Pirate Dander's here," said Humphrey.

"I'll just say 'Love you and see you very soon'," said Sal.

Joe and Francie took Humphrey to see the message being sent off, and Vivi rolled up to the table. "There's news, Lysander. And linner, thanks to a neighbour."

Lysander and Sal sat down. "I'm listening," he said.

"The prisoners are going to be moved. On Hallowmas Day. We don't know where to, but they're going by dirigible so it's not nearby. We have to rescue them soon. We have seven days at the most."

"Seven days!" Lysander bounced up to squat, frog-style, on the bench. "Everything's happening at once. You've got the Land Court case the day after and I'm doing the big fireworks show on Hallowmas Eve. Too many things. Too many things!"

"But we have to rescue them."

"We absolutely do. Seven days."

"And we have this." She laid Francie's plan of the prison in front of him.

Lysander studied it for a full minute. "With this," he announced, "we could finally have an uprising."

Chapter Fourteen

A Genius Idea

They were doing the dishes after dinner and Humphrey was squealing about the hot water that magically came out of a tap in the scullery when Vivi came in. "Pigeon post for you."

Sal dropped her tea towel and snatched up the scrap of paper. "It's from Ma, sending love!"

They passed the paper round. Joe was relieved to see Ma's familiar handwriting. It looked a bit shaky, but then she was doing doll-sized writing on the thinnest paper in the world.

"I've just had a genius idea," said Hessa. She paused. "Yes! Definitely genius. I know how to send a message to our parents. We've got to go back to the prison, now, before it's too dark. I'll just get some things from the shed."

Humphrey was desperate to try the hot rain, and Sal was happy to stay with him and keep discussing plans with Vivi and Lysander.

Hessa, Joe and Francie changed back into their dark clothes and set off. They reached their lookout just before sunset. The shadows of the buildings stretched across the plain, then disappeared as the sun dropped behind the mountains.

A bell rang. Lights went on. Through his telescope Joe saw candles and lamplight flickering in windows, and the lamps outside the buildings being lit.

They crawled quietly over the rocky slope facing the prison, preparing it for their messages by pulling out big weeds and throwing them to one side. They waited until the lanterns left the watchtowers, and the watchtowers went dark. They listened to the noises carrying in the chilly air: the clatter of a crate of bottles being set down, the bell ringing, voices calling and loud, persistent barking from the dogs.

Then it was time.

Hessa levered the lid off a pail of white paint, dipped her brush in and painted letters two metres high.

♥ LOVE YOU MUM AND DAD. SOON! HT

She went over the letters again, painting grass, stones and earth. The letters got smaller and more irregular as she went, but the message was surely readable for miles.

Then Francie painted a message for Pa underneath. They'd had a lot of discussion about what to say. It had to be short, and not give anything away to Custodians or warders. In the end they decided on:

♥ WE ARE HERE. BREADY! SJF&H XXXX

The fact that their message was underneath Hessa's would tell Pa that they were working with the Terrabynds, and "Bready" was what Pa used to write on his notes. It meant "Be ready".

"I'm ready," said Joe as they walked back to the house. "I'm ready for anything."

Bright morning on the hillside. Messages clear. Four warders chopping at them with spades.

Turn, fly over prison to back entrance. Message? Message?

Yard. Dogs prowling the long wall. Buildings.

Where's Pa? Has he put a message somewhere? Roofs, windows, warders leaving their building. Nothing, nothing.

Prisoners. Filing out on male side of prison. Round and round. More and more men. Too many faces have big beards and side whiskers. Where is Pa? Are you Pa? Are you?

Follow them around the circuit. Look for colours, shapes. Around again. This time, letters in the dirt! "E M P". Doesn't spell anything. Ahead, a man pauses, bends, ties bootlace, but when he walks on, "I R E" scratched in sand. Is IRE a word? What about Empire?

Something about this man—the slope of his shoulders, head angled like a listening bird. It could be.

But if it is him, it's a thinner Pa. His beard is grey. Do people change so much in a year?

His face is shaded by his hat.

Then he looks up at the sky. Pa. Of course it's Pa!

His eyes crinkle, and he smiles up at the sky, all around. Sends out love, patience, calm. He's still Pa, and Pa means safety.

He looks down again and scrapes "H O T" in the dirt with his boot. Then, "E L". Empire Hotel. Once more around circuit. More letters appear. "O D O" followed by "P A. X X".

Chapter Fifteen

Emp ire Hot el Odo

When Francie sat up, Joe could see straight away that she was happy. "You saw Pa!"

Francie beamed at him.

Vivi had been top and tailing beans, very grumpily, even though Humphrey was lining them up so she could slice through several at once. She threw her knife down and wiped her hands when they joined her at the table. "Thank goodness. Did you find anything?"

Francie drew Pa, and the message he'd scratched in the dirt: *Emp ire Hot el Odo Pa. XX.*

They all shrieked and talked at once. This was so exciting—Joe realised that he hadn't actually believed it would work.

Sal listed their questions:

1) Is there an Empire Hotel in Cruxcia? (Vivi)

2) Did Pa stay there? (Sal)

3) Or Waldo Watkins? (Joe)

4) What is an Odo? (Humphrey)

"We have to go and find out," said Sal. "If there's an Empire Hotel, and if so, ask them if Pa stayed there. And if he did, ask what's happened to his things—his rucksack and valise."

"They should still have them," said Vivi. "The rules say a hotel must keep all lost property for a minimum of one year, after which the articles may be sold to defray costs if outstanding bills remain unpaid."

"Wow!" said Sal.

Hessa grinned. "Vivi knows all the regulations by heart."

It had to be Joe who went. Francie needed to nap and Sal was going to get everything organised for the mapping expedition—so they could concentrate on the escape plan. There were only six days until Hallowmas.

Joe wandered clockwise around the town, and asked some children if they knew where the Empire Hotel was. They didn't, but a small boy offered to take him to the Mendalwar View Hotel. He kept going. He joined a game of football with some other children. When he'd saved two goals and scored one, he asked about the Empire Hotel. They pointed down a side road. That easy.

A six-storey building, much wider than most in Cruxcia, had a gold sign with EMPIRE HOTEL in curly writing above its heavy door, with GTC underneath. The answer to question one was, yes.

He pushed the door open and crossed the marble floor of the lobby. The receptionist didn't look up from his writing.

"Excuse me?"

The man looked over the top of his pince-nez. "Yes?" He gave the word three syllables.

Joe recited the words he'd been practising all the way. "Excuse me, my name is Joseph Santander. I think my father Leopold Santander stayed here some months ago? He had to leave suddenly, and I believe he left some belongings. I've come to collect them."

"Santander? No, we have nothing belonging to Mr Santander here." The man's voice was chillier than an icicle.

"But you haven't even checked! Can you look in your left luggage or lost property, please?"

"I don't believe we've ever had a customer of that name." He clicked his fingers to a boy in a maroon and gold uniform.

"Oh." Joe felt sick. What now? "Sorry to bother you," he managed to say. Had they misunderstood Pa's message?

The desk man said to the uniformed boy: "Odo, show this young man out."

Odo! Joe crossed back over the shiny floor. As he went out of the door, he whispered, "Odo?"

The boy murmured, "Back door. Wait for me."

An alley ran alongside the hotel to the back where a couple of stabled horses were exchanging snorts and whinnies with a brewery horse harnessed to a cart. Two men were using poles with spikes on the end to manoeuvre barrels of beer off the cart and down a ramp into the hotel cellars. It was all very interesting.

After a few minutes Odo came out of the back door. "I'm Lammy Odo. You Mr Santander's boy?"

"Yes, I'm Joe." Odo touched his forehead and Joe did the same. "Pa was arrested."

"I know," said Odo. "Quick, come on." He opened a small

door marked STAFF ONLY. He paused at the bottom of a dark staircase and listened. They didn't talk as they climbed to the very top of the building then tiptoed along a low, windowless corridor.

"Only night staff are meant to be up here in the daytime," Odo whispered as they entered a small room with four beds. One of them had a boy in it who turned over groggily and mumbled something. "He's on night shift." Odo told the boy to go back to sleep. Then he pushed one of the empty beds up against the next one and crouched down in the gap. "Have you got a knife?"

Joe flicked out the largest blade of his precious pocket knife. Odo pushed it between two floorboards and levered one up. He reached down and pulled out—Pa's map tube! He gave the knife back to Joe and passed him the tube. It rattled.

"Oh my goodness—thank you!"

Odo pressed the floorboard back in place and stood up. "That's all. His other things, nightshirt, toothbrush and so on, I put in a bag and took to the prison for Mr Santander."

"What?" Joe whispered. "That's really kind. Why did you help him?"

"Because they're kind men, him and old Mr Waldo. They talked to me. About maps, and Mr Santander told me about his children, and how much he missed you." Odo spoke fast but quietly as he pulled the bed back into place. "When your father overheard Mr Manager-Sir say that I broke a lamp and had to give *all my wages* for half a year, Mr Santander said, 'No, it was I, not Odo, who broke the lamp. So very sorry.' And he paid."

"Had Pa broken it?"

"No. There was no broken lamp. Mr Manager-Sir just likes money." Odo pulled a face. "I should be in the kitchen. We'll go down."

Joe followed along the corridor as Odo continued his whispered story. "Mr Santander was eating breakfast when the Custodians came. He mumbled 'Maps, my room' to me when they marched him past."

An angry voice was coming up the stairs.

"Uh-oh." Odo turned and urged Joe back into the bedroom, where he threw the window open. "Out—quick."

There was a tiny platform of a fire escape outside the window. Joe scrambled out and Odo followed, crouching low and pulling the window down behind them.

"Down." The fire escape was a series of wooden ladders from one balcony to the next. Odo had obviously done this before and survived, which was good to know as some of the rungs were broken and the whole contraption wobbled. At least this side of the hotel was in deep shade so they wouldn't be obvious from the yard. Odo went down one level. Joe dropped the tube to him and climbed down himself, then Odo handed Joe the tube and went down the next ladder.

Odo kept talking quietly as they descended. "So, I took the pass key, and in Mr Santander's room, I found this tube. Also, his valise. I know what they're allowed in the prison because my father has been locked up for two years, for throwing an egg at Moustache Man."

"Two years for throwing an egg?"

"Old Mundle bought a horse off my father and said his

paymaster would come next day with the money. But no one came. So, my father went to the governor's house to demand the money or his horse back. And the butler says, 'His Excellency understands that the horse is a gift, an excellent gift. He thanks you.' *Gift?* Nothing less likely! So, when my father saw Mundle out riding his horse, he threw an egg. So now, prison. Should have thrown a horseshoe, I reckon."

They had to hang from the last platform and jump. Odo went first, then Joe passed the map tube down and dropped to the ground.

"I hope you don't get into trouble. Thank you so, so much, Odo. Dasa. Freedom for Cruxcians!"

"Freedom for Cruxcians! Soon. When all the adults get out of prison, we'll have a big party." Odo laughed. He hoisted a crate of bottles from the brewer's cart nonchalantly onto his shoulder and disappeared down the ramp into the cellar.

Chapter Sixteen

Maps and Plans

Hessa had just finished ladling hot chutney into a row of jars when Joe arrived waving the tube. Sal recognised it immediately. "You got it, you got it!"

Francie took Humphrey's hands and swung him round.

Joe levered the cap off and held the tube at an angle. Something slid out—Pa's *compass*! He clutched it to his chest and blinked back tears, then he hung it round his neck. "I'll look after it until he's free."

They all piled close to see what else was in the tube. The table outside was daubed with chutney stickiness, and the table inside was covered with Vivi's papers, so Hessa suggested they use Tash and Taliesin's bed. Sal eased the roll of paper out and Hessa, Joe and Francie each held a corner.

It was a large map, with Cruxcia at the bottom and the Afa valley going right into the mountains where the river began. The top half of the map was sketchy and unfinished, but the bottom half was colourful. It showed the farms and buildings, and the boundaries of all the fields, paddocks and orchards, as far as a road bridge over the river.

"Isn't this what you wanted us to map?" said Joe. "It's already done!"

"Thank goodness." Sal was overwhelmed with relief. "We just need to finish it—fill in that top section."

There was some smaller paper in the tube. Sal couldn't reach it, but Humphrey's little arm fitted in. "There's two." He slid the first one out. It was headed SPECIFICATIONS.

Sal read: "*The map for the Land Claim Court must show the Afa river basin from Cruxcia to the watershed, must include all land ownership and must be signed over a seal by an accredited member of the International Society of Mapmakers.*"

"Over a seal?" said Joe. "What's that mean?"

"Brurck brurck!" Humph flapped imaginary flippers. They'd seen seals at New Coalhaven.

Sal laughed. "A wax seal. Ma's got one in her bits and bobs bag. She's an accredited member." She read on. "*In addition, the Governor requires two further maps for his personal use.*

Map Two must show the plain beyond Cruxcia for twenty kilometres in each direction.

Map Three must be of the river basin, including, and upstream of, the land called 'Mina Mendalwar'. The only necessary detail to be a single contour line, at an elevation measured from Mina Mendalwar's peak, minus 30 metres."

"Can you get the last one out, Humph?" Joe held the tube and Humph fished out the next piece of paper. It was a map of the valley with a line around it. "So this is Map Three, with the contour line. But why?"

Francie was waving. She took Sal's hand and led her to the shed. At the back, Francie dragged the tool bag from under the sacks, undid the clasps, and took out Ma's map tube.

"Oh clever, clever Francie—of course! Map Two. Waldo Watkins's map that Ma bought from the map shop. The one Tall and Short saw her buying."

She unrolled it on the bed. It was as she remembered it. Mountains in the top right-hand corner with a few place names, Cruxcia at the base of the mountains, and the routes across the plain. And something else she hadn't noticed before. A faint pencilled square. "Look! Is that the prison?"

"Is there a prison here?" Humphrey looked frightened.

"Um—" Sal looked at Joe. What were they going to tell Humphrey? "There is," she said in an offhand voice.

"Is this map unfinished too, or is it blank because there's nothing in this bit?" asked Joe.

"It's not nothing," Vivi protested. "It's where the Fanafi live. They live in tents and move around the plains, collecting minerals, bark and berries. All the ingredients Pi uses to make medicine and Taliesin uses to make colours."

"I like tents," said Humphrey.

"Why does Mundle want these two maps?" said Vivi. "What does it mean?"

Everyone had questions, but no answers. Sal turned back to the map of the valley that was half finished. She touched where it changed to pencil. "How long would it take to walk to here?"

Hessa knew. "Where the road goes over the river is Prontin Bridge, about four hours' walk. Then it's another three hours to the turnoff and another hour to Bereff Stonch. It's an all-day walk from here."

"What's Bereff Stonch?"

"It's old Cruxcian, meaning a flat place for sheep. It's a derelict cottage in the mountains—you could stay there," said Vivi. "Finish the map from there?"

"Yes!" Hessa exclaimed. "I love going there. I'll take you."

"Me too, me too—I'm coming, aren't I, Hessa?" said Humphrey.

Joe hugged Francie. "At last! We're going into the mountains."

Sal was torn. Once, she'd have jumped at the chance to go mapping with the others, but she really wanted to stay and plan with Vivi. She knew she had to go.

It was too late to leave that evening, so they agreed to an early start. Sal could do whatever measuring was needed for Francie to finish Pa's map.

"Tomorrow there'll only be five more days to go," said Sal.

"Away three days," Vivi calculated. "We'll still have two nights to do the rescue."

"We'll need travelling supplies," said Hessa.

"We've got money for you." Sal handed over her purse full of coins.

"It's heavy! Can I get a few treats for Vivi too? I'll see if Stracky can take me to the market."

Francie let Humphrey help her feed the chickens and collect the eggs while Sal and Joe pulled all their belongings out of the shed.

They didn't have a donkey, so Sal would have to pull the altimeter.

When Vivi saw it she was scornful. "You can't pull it like that. Give it to me. I'll get Stracky's father to make you a yoke. He can make anything—he made Doris." She tied the altimeter across her lap and disappeared up the lane.

No donkeys meant they'd have to carry everything they needed themselves, and they couldn't expect Humphrey to carry much. Sal packed her ruler and dividers, compass, knife and pencils, and rolled the maps into Ma's tube, which was lighter than Pa's. She packed extra warm clothes for herself and Humphrey, and that was all she could do until the morning.

Stracky's father returned the altimeter an hour later with poles attached to either side of the shaft, and a soft leather strap between them. When Sal fitted the yoke over her shoulders, she was relieved to find that she could walk with her hands free and the altimeter followed her without wobbling. It still wouldn't be easy over rough ground, but it was a million times better than pulling it with her hands.

One more job to do, and that was to tell Humphrey before he heard from someone else.

He was practising jumping off the steps. "Watch me! I can do four steps."

"I need to tell you something." Sal explained about the bad governor, and the prison, and how Lysander's parents, and Vivi and Hessa's parents and Pa were all in there. "But Pa is alive and well, and we're going to get him out," she said quickly.

"I'll save him!" Humph swiped the air with an imaginary

sword. "Me and Pirate Dander will do rescuing!" He raced off round the yard, slicing through enemies and dicing them into tiny pieces. "I'm coming, Pa. I'm coming!"

Chapter Seventeen

A Secret, Risky Meeting

Joe lay in his sleeping bag watching the stars creep across the sky. The Big Fish was gradually coming into view over the flowering bushes that grew in pots along the roof. It was standing on its tail, whereas on the Race it had been more horizontal. He trained his telescope on the eye of the fish, the brightest star in the constellation. He knew, and could see through the telescope, that it was really two stars, not one.

Down in the road, a dog barked. Somewhere, a door opened and shut. Frogs sang. Then he heard a rustle much closer. He sat up. Hessa was slithering out of her sleeping bag and putting her sandals on.

"Where are you going?" he whispered.

"Just got to go and meet someone."

"I can't sleep. Can I come?"

"If you're very quiet."

Joe hadn't taken his clothes off, so all he had to do was put his boots on, and his jacket.

Vivi was waiting in Doris. She nodded to Joe. "Good, you can help Hessa push. Not yet, though."

There was enough light from the moon and stars as they walked along the empty road towards town. They turned off onto a side road that was steep and rutted. Joe and Hessa took a handle each of the wheelchair and added their weight to Vivi's arm-pumping. Joe wondered how Vivi managed usually.

"Usually," puffed Vivi, as if she'd read his mind, "I can go kilometres without help. But I stay on good roads. Lysander is an idiot."

Before Joe could ask her to explain, Hessa whispered "Shala, Stracky" into the darkness. Just ahead, a figure sat very still, back against a wall. His arms were around a large dog, which growled menacingly as they passed.

"Stracky's guarding the old quarry for us," said Hessa. "His dog Luna's so clever; she barks whenever a Custodian's coming."

Joe shivered with nervous excitement. Not only a midnight expedition but a secret, risky meeting.

Ahead, the quarry was like a bite taken out of the hill by a giant. The exposed rock glowed pale and mysterious in the moonlight. The quarry was tiered, like a theatre, and blocks of stone lay around. Sitting on the blocks were—Joe tried to count—at least twenty children and teenagers. More. Some had lanterns; one or two candles flickered. He was surprised that they were all allowed out so late, until he remembered that many were living without parents.

Vivi rolled up to Lysander, who was still wearing his pirate scarf. "Lysander Santander Faraxarendrel Klim, you have the brain of a peacock. A quarry by moonlight may be romantic in a story, but in real life the road is so difficult I can only assume you hoped I wouldn't come."

Lysander looked embarrassed. "I'm really sorry, Vivi. I didn't think. Hello Joe, Hessa."

"Think, next time."

"I'm glad you're here. I'll start the meeting." Lysander called for hush. "Shala, everyone. It's good so many of us could come. As you know, the trouble has started! Miners' tents have gone up, and big machinery has been unloaded at the bottom of Mina Mendalwar. I called this meeting in order to discuss how to stop them."

"Wait a minute," said Vivi, "can we find out what societies are here?"

"Oh, right." Lysander started calling out the names. "Cloth makers? Yes. Metal workers? Clay workers? Yes, entertainers? Lilja, good; wood workers? Max is here from paper workers. Market workers? Scholars, carers, farmers? Growers?"

Vivi nodded at a boy called Madoc and asked how he was.

"We're managing, but Etta misses Mama a lot. We both do."

"I hope she'll be out of prison very soon."

Vivi asked everyone to come closer and sit where they could all see each other. "So, the Land Court is sitting next week. I'm trying to finish the case many of your parents were working on. The case to prove that the land in the valley belongs to all of us."

Vivi pointed to Joe. "This boy is the son of Leopold Santander, the mapmaker who's in prison. He and his sisters are making the map to go with my submission. We'll need lots of help to get it ready, especially from people with small, neat handwriting. But things have changed with the arrival of the miners' camp. Lysander is going to talk about that."

Lysander stood up and spun round theatrically. His eyes flashed in the moonlight. "At the moment there are just a few miners, but we've heard there are many more workmen on their way. We want them to leave, and leave because they choose to—without violence. They're from Eronya and only speak Eronyan, apart from their foreman. He said they've been promised a lot of money to come and work here. We know what a mean liar Moustache Man is. I told him they'll probably have to pay the GTC for all the food they've eaten, and their transport and rent for the tents, but he didn't believe me.

"So we have to persuade them to go. I warned the foreman about Hallowmas, and that sometimes our ancestors rise out of their graves. Did he understand? Don't know, but he did say that the miners hate sleeping so close to a graveyard.

"As you know, my father's in prison so I'm doing the fireworks this year. It won't just be fireworks; I'm planning a show to terrify the miners. Before the actual night they'll see mysterious lights and hear strange noises. Small performances of scariness to make them nervous." Lysander was sounding and looking very dramatic. "Leading up to a huge and brilliant performance that will scare the miners so badly, they'll flee to Porto Pearls without even changing their undies!"

Everyone cheered and clapped.

Lysander opened his arms wide. "We need everyone. It's going to be the biggest, most exciting Hallowmas ever. But we need our whisper-chain. One person from each society must come to the pyrotechnic workshop every morning to receive their instructions." Lysander put up his hand to shush the excited buzz. "Also, you must keep all this secret until Hallowmas. No telling *any* adults in case the GTC's spies find out." Lysander drew his finger across his lips. "Agreed?"

Everyone copied him. "Agreed," they called back softly.

"One other thing," said Vivi. "The Cowboys have been painting red marks like crosses on the ground—" She stopped. They could hear ferocious barking. "Custodians. Go home. Don't be seen. Voh'mah berrin. And put your lanterns out."

They scattered. Joe heard scuffling and rustling as most of the children bolted from the quarry. A few ran to the back and started scrambling up the tiers of rock. There was nothing to hide behind; they'd be visible in the moonlight until they reached the top. Hessa and Joe pushed Vivi out of the quarry and into the lane and Lysander followed.

"If it's the Custodians Humph was sick on, they'll recognise us," hissed Hessa. "Quick, give us a leg-up, Lysander. You stay with Vivi."

Lysander gave Hessa, then Joe, a leg-up onto the high stone wall that bordered the lane. Joe heard grumbling voices coming nearer, and Luna's barks, then dark shadows appeared behind a bright lantern. Hessa jumped off the wall into darkness, and Joe followed.

It was further than he'd guessed, and he jarred his wrists and ankles as he landed, but everything still worked. There was just enough moonlight to see that they were in a large paddock, with a high wall all around and a gate on the far side. A few cows were grazing in the middle. Over the wall, the Custodians demanded to know what Vivi and Lysander were doing.

"We're just out for walk," said Lysander. "Sir."

"A walk? At this time of night?"

"We have to come at night because Vivi is sick. She can't go out in the day. Sunshine makes her eyes bleed. It's very bad."

"And who are you?" asked another voice.

"Her brother."

Joe heard a splutter and imagined Vivi exploding with irritation. Lysander was acting as if Vivi couldn't speak for herself. Now Vivi had to go along with him or the Custodians would be suspicious.

She spluttered some more and Lysander said, "Poor Vivi, you're drooling. Hang on, I'll just dry your mouth." Lysander was enjoying himself.

Joe moved—and put his hand in a cow pat. Yuck! He tried to wipe it off on the grass.

"What was that?" said a guard's voice.

"What was what?" asked Lysander. "You mean the cows?"

Cows! Joe crept away from the wall, pulling out grass as he went. Hessa followed him, making little snorts. She was trying not to laugh. When he'd gone a little way, Joe became bolder. "Moo," he called. "Moo-moo."

That did it. Hessa collapsed full length on the grass and buried her face in her hands, her body heaving and feet kicking in not-quite-silent hysterics.

"Moo," she whispered. "Moo," and laughed harder.

It was catching. Joe clamped his lips with his teeth but a great snort escaped through his nose. "Moo!"

The real cows were staring in their direction. They started to amble over. Surely cows weren't this big? And didn't have such huge horns? Maybe they were buffalo. Or bulls.

They were between Joe and the gate. "Hessa," Joe hissed. "We need to move."

"Mooo-ve!" Hessa spluttered, but she got to her feet.

Joe tried to remember what you were supposed to do in a field with a bull. Stand still? Walk calmly? Run for your life? Hessa was sprinting silently towards the gate. Joe tried to skirt around the beasts, but they spread out to cut him off. They waved their heads up and down, as though about to charge.

"Come on!" Hessa called in a loud whisper.

"Good bulls," Joe murmured as he shuffled forward. "Such beautiful horns. But also sharp. Please don't jab me. I'll just slip between you two, very nice to have met you. See you again soon. Bye-ee."

He was past them. He expected galloping hooves or a horn in his back, but when he glanced around, they were grazing again.

Hessa was sitting on the gate. "That was so funny!" she said. "Vivi's going to kill Lysander!"

Hadn't Hessa noticed how scared he was of the bulls? He told her. She laughed harder. "Didn't you notice their great milk sacs?"

Joe felt his cheeks go hot.

Vivi was waiting further up the lane. She'd ordered Lysander to get out of her sight. Joe was bursting with questions, but he was suddenly too tired; they could wait until morning. There was only one that felt urgent. "Is Lysander really called Lysander Santander?"

"Lysander Santander Faraxarendrel (which is a plant good for lighting fires) Klim, showman of Cruxcia. He really is," said Vivi.

"Is he related to us then?"

Vivi snorted. "I hope not, for your sake."

Chapter Eighteen

The Road to Bereff Stonch

It didn't take long to get the last things ready. Humphrey was big enough now to carry his own rucksack. Sal put his jacket and hat into it and rolled his sleeping bag up with her own. Francie and Joe took his spare clothes. Joe sent a last pigeon to Ma saying they were going for a small adventure and wouldn't be sending any messages for a couple of days.

Hessa put a thick leather jerkin over her shirt. "For Magnus's claws," she explained. "I can probably carry him on my gauntlet for an hour, but not all day. He's better on my shoulder."

"Why's Magnus coming?" asked Sal. She could see that Joe wasn't keen on Magnus either.

"He could be useful." Vivi put a tin box on the table. "There's his meat."

"Who's Magnus?" whispered Humphrey, who was still a bit shy of Vivi.

"Another bird," said Joe. "A big one, with talons."

When Magnus emerged from his shed towering regally above Hessa, Humphrey hid behind Joe, and Carrot burrowed into Sal's jacket pocket. Only her head poked out.

They loaded up. Joe strapped the theodolite and tripod across his rucksack and the coil of rope on top.

"We don't need that," said Sal. "This isn't a proper expedition, you know."

Joe looked hurt. "Don't you remember what Pa said? *Always carry the longest rope you can, just in case.* Well, I'm doing what he said, even if you're not."

"It's stupid. It's just more to carry," Sal snapped, and wished she hadn't. She got waspish when she was worried, and there was a lot to worry about. A huge bird that could slice someone's face off with one swipe of his claws, a sick mother and a little brother who'd been sick and might not be able to walk far, a map to finish in record time, and a father who needed rescuing before he was whisked off in a dirigible to who-knew-where—everything was worrying.

Hessa headed out the gate with a brightly coloured Cruxcian backpack and Magnus on her shoulder. Covering his head was a leather hood with a little feather on top.

Francie carried the map tube and her drawing equipment.

Stracky was waiting on the road with Luna. He'd volunteered to follow five minutes behind them, so if any Cowboys or Custodians came along, they'd hear her barking. Humphrey squatted to pat Luna.

"This is so kind of you," said Sal.

"I'm going up the valley anyway, to pick fruit," said Stracky.

They said goodbye to him and followed the road along the river. With its gentle curves and slopes, Stracky was soon out of sight.

"Why's he picking fruit?" Joe asked Hessa.

"It's the harvest holidays, when everyone helps. Except this year, with so many in prison, it's not very organised."

Sal adjusted the yoke on her shoulders. It was strange being the donkey pulling the altimeter, but the harness was comfortable. She was glad Vivi had thought of it.

"I saw Stracky last night, too," said Joe. He told Sal and Francie about his adventure with the other children, about the whisper-chain and Lysander's show. "He's going to do an amazing performance with fireworks. It'll get rid of the miners—they'll be right underneath and they'll be so scared they'll run to the Sky Worff to catch the next dirigible home. There'll be strange noises and lights. Lysander called them Small Performances of Scariness. And on Hallowmas night, there'll be fireworks and ghosts and noise. Loads of children will be in it."

Sal thought about everything she was discovering about this place. In spite of the arrests and imprisonments, there were lots of good things about Cruxcia.

The road was busy with carts coming from the farms laden with crates of fruit and vegetables. Every cart towed a cloud of dust from the dry road, so they were soon filthy.

"It's like this in summer." Hessa was tying a large handkerchief over her mouth and nose, "but soon the rains will come. Mud is much worse."

Sal preferred dust: the altimeter would be impossible to

manage in mud. There was something else, though—not mud, but enormous poos. Ahead of them, two teams of oxen pulled heavily laden carts so slowly, the children were able to overtake.

Humph kept running ahead then running back. He got braver about Magnus, and soon he was walking beside Hessa while she told him about birds of prey and how she and Vivi had trained Magnus.

"Why doesn't he fly away?"

"Because I've got his jesses—these leather cords—clipped to his ankles."

Humphrey peered closer. "Why's he wearing that helmet?"

"It's a hood. Vivi sewed it. It sends Magnus to sleep because he thinks it's night time. It keeps him calm when we're travelling."

Carrot got braver, too. She perched on Humphrey's shoulder and said, "Yoo-hoo! Big bird!" But Magnus was too dignified, or too fast asleep, to react.

Joe smiled. "It seems like years since we were doing this."

"It's a hundred and sixteen days," said Sal, who knew without calculating. "I wish we still had Beckett with us."

They'd never have finished the race without Beckett and his skills at finding food and cooking. They'd needed everyone's skills.

People in the orchards picking fruit called "shala" as they went past, and they called back.

Vivi had asked them to check the Cowboys' marks, and Hessa led them up a lane to the middle of a goat paddock. A boy from the farm showed them where the Cowboys had scraped away grass in the shape of an X, then painted the ground red.

"X marks the spot!" said Humphrey. "Prob'ly treasure."

Joe unstrapped the theodolite. Humph was appalled to discover that no one had brought a spade. "Everyone knows about X marks the spot," he howled. "You do digging, not stupid measuring, when you find an X."

Carrot flew onto Humphrey's head. "W, X, Why? Why not."

Sal ignored Humph and Carrot and opened the altimeter. In it was the mechanism that made a dot on the paper roll every hundred metres to show their height above sea level as they went along. She made notes. It was as she thought. "Time to move on," she called.

Humphrey was sulking, Joe was eating windfall mandarins, Hessa was deep in conversation with the boy from the farm, and Francie was being mobbed by small goats with gentle faces that were scrambling over one another to have their droopy ears stroked.

"Come on!" she yelled again. It was like organising chickens. "I'm going." She set off down the hill. How had they ever got across the mountains all together?

Eventually they were all back on the road. Joe tossed everyone a mandarin.

"You know the map Moustache Man wanted, with just one line on it? Map Three?" Sal gave some peel to Carrot. "Well, the cross we just saw is exactly on that line. I think the Cowboys have been making crosses to mark where the line goes. Round the valley, thirty metres lower than the peak of Mina Mendalwar. Which means we don't need to check any more crosses."

"Excellent. Straight on to Bereff Stonch then," said Hessa.

Before long, Humphrey shouted, "Luna's barking!"

Sal had forgotten all about Stracky and Luna. There were definitely low, snarly barks far behind them. Hessa took off Magnus's hood and released his jessses. "Fly, Magnus, as high as you can!" The hawk soared up and disappeared into the clouds.

"In case it's them, into the trees—quick." Sal grabbed Humphrey's hand and ran across the verge towards the nearest orchard.

The ground disappeared.

Sal was lying, face down and winded, with the altimeter on top of her. She couldn't move. "Humph? Humph!" She turned her head: there was his knee. He was underneath her, twisted and still. She tried to lift her weight off him. "Humph!"

For a horrible moment she thought he was dead. Then a foot scraped down her chest, hard. "Ow! Joe!" she called. "Get the altimeter off me." She could hear scrabbling and some of the weight was lifted. She tried to roll sideways but met a wall of dirt. Was she in a grave?

"You all right?" said Joe's voice.

Sal tried to shrug the harness off her shoulders. "No, I'm not."

"You ran into the ditch. The altimeter's tangled with your rucksack, hang on."

"They're coming," Hessa called urgently.

Next thing, Hessa and Francie were in the ditch, too. Hessa freed the altimeter and Francie helped Humphrey scramble out from under Sal.

"You all right, Humph?" asked Joe. "Anywhere hurting?"

"Sal squashed me. I'm all flat."

"Sorry." Sal managed to turn and sit up. The bottom of the ditch was wet and muddy—and so was she.

"Keep down and quiet." Hessa peered through the weeds that had hidden the ditch. "Cowboys."

They flattened themselves as the horses approached. The thumping inside Sal seemed as loud as the hoofbeats.

"Shhh, they're stopping," Hessa whispered.

Joe held his finger across his lips and Humphrey nodded and screwed his eyes tight shut as well as his mouth.

"Which way did that bird go?" Cody Cole's voice boomed out.

"There! Get it!" a Cowboy shouted, and a gun went off very close. Everyone in the ditch jumped, then froze.

"Damn. Missed. After that bird!" The horses galloped off.

"They shot at Magnus," said Joe in horror.

"He'll be fine," Hessa said firmly. "Magnus is un-shootable."

They stood up cautiously and peered round. The horses were already out of sight. But Humph squealed, "They're coming back!" They all ducked down again, seconds before the Cowboys returned. The hoofbeats slowed and another gunshot echoed round the valley.

The horses stopped, and a Cowboy swore. Sal could just see their heads through the undergrowth. "That bird's as sneaky as the Cruxcians."

Their grunts of agreement turned to screams as Magnus dived from out of thin air. Before the Cowboys could lift their guns, he'd swooped on Cody Cole, snatched his hat in his talons and flown off with it.

"Noooooo!" bellowed Cody Cole. "Boiling's too good for it!

Stop that bird." Hooves galloped away towards Cruxcia.

"That was sensational," said Sal. "You're sure he'll be all right? Magnus, I mean?"

"He's leading them away from us," said Hessa. "Clever bird."

"We'll give them five minutes." Sal counted to three hundred.

Stracky caught up with them and they thanked Luna for her excellent barking, then he turned off to pick pears and they waved goodbye.

They walked on for a while. Joe and Hessa were discussing whether, if they had a snack now, it would count as late morning tea or early lunch, when Magnus swooped in low under the trees and landed on Hessa's arm. She rewarded him with something from his food tin.

"What's he eating?" asked Humphrey.

"A dead mouse," said Hessa.

"Dead!" Carrot shrieked and tried to hide under Francie's hair.

"Can I see?" asked Humph. "Are there more dead mice in there?"

Hessa took the lid off. "No, but there's a chick without its head and a rabbit heart."

Humphrey peered. "Does Magnus like eating that stuff?"

"Loves it. Wild hawks eat birds mainly. They snatch them out of the sky with their fierce claws. They're the fastest fliers in the world."

Blood dribbled down Magnus's beak.

"Revolting," said Sal. "But I'm glad he's on our side."

The road crossed lots of small streams that flowed into the river and Humph collected sticks to hand out at each bridge.

They dropped their sticks in and raced over the road to see whose was fastest.

"You win again, Humph. Seven to you, three to Hessa and Francie and one to me," said Joe. "I think you may have found another special skill."

Humphrey was fighting wild flowers along the verge with his stick when he noticed a cream and maroon sign close to the water.

"Look! It says Ma, then X-marks-the-spot."

"Good reading," said Sal.

"Max Ext?" said Joe. "Is it a name?"

Hessa said she knew a Max, but no one in Cruxcia was called Ext. Maybe the sign had been put there as a prank. Maybe some of it was missing. But it looked new and a familiar shade of brownish-red. It had to be something to do with the Cowboys.

"Max usually stands for maximum," said Sal. "It could be short for Maximum Extent."

"What's that mean?" asked Hessa.

"It's the furthest point of something. As far as it goes," said Sal.

"As far as what goes?" asked Joe.

"No idea yet," said Sal. She borrowed a blue pencil from Francie and made a tiny blue "x" on the scroll inside the altimeter. She'd think about it as they walked along.

The road grew steeper. They came to Prontin Bridge and crossed the river.

"This is where the map stops," said Hessa.

The road became more of a track as it wound up and up into the mountains. After a steep stretch they stopped for a rest and a snack. Francie put a hand to her ear. Listen.

There were strange noises ahead: whistles, barks and a thunderous rumbling. They stood warily and looked around. There was nowhere to hide. The sounds grew louder, then hundreds of sheep came careering around the bend in the track. Carrot shrieked and flew over them to the safety of a tree.

They stood still while the sheep streamed past, driven down the valley by a boy and a girl and four sheepdogs. The girl's whistled instructions sent a dog racing after a sheep that was looking for a private route to the river. The boy sent another dog sprinting around the mob to stop them spilling through a gap in the trees.

"They're bringing the sheep down for the winter," Hessa said, "before the winter rain. They'll bring them back up in spring." She knew the girl from school. She shouted to her, and the girl called back, but couldn't stop to talk. "She doesn't know anything about the sign—it must be new, and she says there's rain coming."

When they were far enough past the dogs, Joe tried out the calls he'd heard. "Coo-rup, bay-o, bay-o." And with index fingers in her mouth, Francie made the whistle. Francie never spoke. She sometimes laughed, and occasionally hummed to herself when she was happy, but this was the first time she'd whistled, and by far the loudest sound she'd ever made. The notes were exactly the ones that had sent the dog towards the river.

"Wow, Francie!" Sal was astonished. She tried to do the whistle, too. She couldn't. Humphrey ran around pretending to be a dog while Francie whistled and laughed.

They were surprised to come up behind another ox cart plodding up the steep track so slowly a snail could overtake it. The tray was piled high with lumpy sacks.

"Where do you think it's going?" asked Sal.

Hessa asked the driver, who just shrugged and smiled and said something incomprehensible.

"I don't know what language that was," she said. "And he didn't understand me. I suppose he's going to Jerval, though this is a long way around."

Finally they arrived at the fork in the track they'd seen on the map. One arm of the signpost pointed back to Cruxcia, one pointed left to Bereff Stonch, and the third pointed right to Jerval.

"Less than an hour to the cottage now," said Hessa.

It was early evening when they reached Bereff Stonch, which was a broad, grassy meadow between steep, thickly forested mountain slopes. The river ran through the meadow, although here it was more of a deep, fast stream.

Hessa pushed the door open. It was dusty inside and the cobwebby windows muted the light. A long time ago it had been

a farmhouse with a family living in it. The big main room had a stove in the middle of one wall with a stack of firewood beside it. Bunks stretched along the walls on either side, with hay-filled sacks for mattresses. Remnants of ancient wallpaper clung to the rough-sawn walls, and cracked old plates were arranged along the shelves of an old dresser.

Hessa put Magnus in a small room that had been a bedroom, and shut the door on him. Carrot cackled. "Bad bird. Ha-ha-ha."

Sal was relieved not to see mouse droppings on the mattresses, or on the big table where Hessa unpacked their food. Humph and Joe went to fetch water from the stream while Francie made a fire in the stove. Hessa took a heavy old frying pan from a cupboard. "Lada tonight, which is eggs, bread and vegetables all fried up together, and I bought a beautiful chimlacanda, a sort of pie, for tomorrow."

"Yum." Sal was very relieved that Hessa had taken charge of the eating side of this expedition.

After dinner, Hessa promised Humphrey a story. Sal spread the maps on the table, took the paper roll out of the altimeter and moved the lantern a little nearer.

Chapter Nineteen

Three Amazing Things

"It's a true story." Hessa poked another log into the woodstove. "It happened to my grandma. It's got three amazing things in it."

Humph burrowed into his sleeping bag. "I'm ready."

"A long, long time ago, Grandma Clarrie lived in this very house with her parents and her brother Wilf. Clarrie and Wilf were twins—like Joe and Francie. They kept goats and sheep, hens and pigs, cows and a horse. When they were ten, Clarrie and Wilf started school in Cruxcia. They stayed with their aunt in town during the week, walked home each Friday afternoon, and back to town on Sunday evenings."

Joe lay down beside Humphrey. "But it took us all day to walk up here!"

"I know. They always ran. They left Cruxcia at lunchtime and were home in time for dinner. One Friday morning, their teacher said, 'A bad storm is coming; you must go now,' even though it was a sunny day."

"How old were they?" asked Joe.

"Twelve, same as you, me and Francie.

"So they start for home, but soon there's no blue sky; everything is grey, and the rain begins. They put on their jackets. The rain falls harder and harder. The ground turns to mud and they slither and slide as they go up the track. Wilf wants to wait in a barn, but Clarrie says, 'No, Mama and Papa will be worried, we must carry on.' They keep going, even though they're wet to their skin and their boots are full of water.

"The river is getting higher, and roaring, and new streams are racing down the valley sides, so loud that Wilf and Clarrie can't hear each other shouting. They link arms to cross the new streams that are already over their knees, and they hurry on."

Humphrey cuddled closer to Joe and whispered, "That's dangerous." He sucked hard on his thumb.

Hessa leaned towards Humphrey. She had a good storytelling voice. "The river is overflowing its banks and creeping towards their path but they're nearly home. Then they see the first amazing thing. Clarrie's cat Tickles is standing on a kitchen chair that goes past, whoosh! down the river. The chair bumps up against a tree that's sticking out of the water. Tickles leaps off it and up into the high branches.

"Clarrie and Wilf go splashing on and soon they see the second amazing thing. Bereff Stonch has turned into a lake! Also, the second-equal amazing thing is Mama pig. The river has reached the pig-house and is taking it for a ride. Mama pig is staring out of the doorway. They manage to grab a corner of the pig-house as it's floating past, push it to dry land and hold it steady while Mama pig scrambles out with six seasick piglets.

"By now, Grandma Clarrie and her brother are very worried about their parents. As they approach their house, the water is nearly to their waists. Then they hear a shout, and there's the third amazing thing. Their mother and father are sitting on top of the roof, with a row of chickens behind them. The twins hurry to the barn and fetch the long hayloft ladder. They float it to the house, and their parents climb down."

"How did they get up there?" asked Joe.

"Great-grandpa stood on a chair on the table and chopped a hole through the ceiling with his axe." Hessa pointed to a faint brown line halfway up the wall. "See? That's where the flood came up to. And that," she pointed to a patch in the ceiling, "covers the hole they escaped through."

"Good story," said Joe.

Humphrey was practically asleep. Francie was lying at the other end of the bunk. Joe felt a nudge from her foot. "What about the animals?" he asked, and Francie's foot nudged again—yes, that was what she wanted to know.

"They found most of them the next day, but they thought they'd lost Tickles the cat as she didn't come home for a month. When she did walk in the kitchen door, she brought three kittens with her."

Hessa made a chewy sort of porridge for breakfast, called farron, then Sal, Joe and Humphrey dressed in their warm exploring clothes and organised the equipment. Joe strapped the theodolite to his rucksack and put the coil of rope over his shoulder. He was excited to be a proper route-finder again, but Sal sighed as she put on the altimeter harness. They meant to climb to the source of the Afa, to measure its altitude and look for more clues.

Hessa would stay behind with Francie, who was going to make her flying nest in the meadow. Magnus would warn Hessa if anyone came near Bereff Stonch—he could perch hidden in a tree for hours, or soar high and spy on anyone approaching. Carrot stayed close to Joe so she wouldn't be left behind. Sal promised Francie they'd be back before dark.

Up and up. Above the apple trees, above the house, above Bereff Stonch where a few sheep still graze. Sal, Joe and Humphrey climbing through the trees. Magnus, high in a pine, turns and stares into her eyes, all-knowing, unblinking.

Down the Afa valley, over the forest towards the orchards, paddocks, farms and fields. A line of ox carts, all going up. Down one side of the river as far as Prontin Bridge. Back up the other side, looking, looking, looking. Along the road to Jerval a little way, road follows stream. But beyond the trees a ridge, and beyond the ridge, something strange. A bald valley. Big wind? Closer. Not wind. Axe. Cleared. Trees cut down. Is that a building? A tower? Here?

Back. Higher and higher above Bereff Stonch. This is how the valley goes, this is how the mountains and valleys fit together.

Back at the house, Francie filled the blank space on the map from Prontin Bridge to Bereff Stonch. with streams and forest, valleys and mountains. She ate the honey sandwich Hessa made for her then curled up on her bunk. When she woke, she went outside to fly again.

Up again, up again, float and spin. The other way now, follow the Afa stream. The forest creeps closer, a green coat hugging the valley. Further, higher, the green coat has a ragged hem, then too high for trees. The valley gets narrower and there at the end is a rope of silver, a gleaming waterfall.

Up, up, and at the top of the waterfall is … snow! A vast sheet of snow; a featherbed snuggled between the mountain peaks.

The River Afa is born from a glacier. The snow is clean and sparkling, dazzling white. Around, around, towards the sun again, but it disappears and a strange wind tugs and shoves. Shiver.

The snow no longer glitters, it's dull, flat, grey. Darkness is swallowing everything.

Back, back, back as quick, quick…

CHAPTER TWENTY

GOING UP

There was a bit of a path along the stream to begin with, but it soon ran out and Joe became the route-finder again. At last. He led Humph and Sal with Carrot flying off on her own investigations then back to squawk at them.

Humphrey sang a song he made up: "I'm a 'sploring boy, with a 'sploring stick and I'm climbing to the top of the world." He used his exploring stick mainly for whacking and poking. Sal had found two strong straight sticks, too, but she used them for balance and support as she hauled the altimeter up behind her.

They followed an overgrown path through the forest—Joe could hear the stream but not see it. There were ferns and creepers to scramble round or over, and Sal often had to stop to untangle the altimeter. As they climbed, the trees changed. They were sparser and smaller, and nothing much grew underneath them. Then they were above the treeline, with a field of rocks ahead, and a cliff beyond. The stream tumbled down the sheer cliff face.

"No," Sal groaned and rubbed her shoulders.

There was no point going straight on. Joe scanned the cliff with his telescope; it dipped at one point, which might mean a way up. The wind was getting stronger. He buttoned up his jacket and Humphrey's too.

Sal abandoned her sticks and carried the tripod, while Joe lifted the back of the altimeter. They picked their way over the stream and around the rocks for nearly an hour. Humphrey leaped from rock to rock and took no notice when Sal growled, "If you slip and break your leg, I'm not carrying you."

They were all going slowly by the time they reached the dip in the cliff, but as Pa always said, *Even going slowly you'll get there in the end.* Joe was pleased—and relieved—to find that he had read the land right. He could see a possible route. They sat and ate bread with strange, salty Cruxcian cheese, then set off again, up a crack in the rock that was like a path: steep, but covered in thick moss, smooth enough for the altimeter to roll over.

It was getting very cold. They were almost at the top when a gust of freezing wind knocked Sal to her knees and nearly bowled Humph back down the mountain. Joe just managed to grab him by his jacket—which only stayed on because, for once, he had kept it buttoned up. Carrot crawled, trembling, into Joe's jacket pocket.

They were all scared.

Sal shouted, "You two stay here. I'll just check the height at the top."

"No! We stick together," Joe yelled back over the wind. "We're nearly there."

So although dark clouds surged and boiled around them, they kept going, and a few minutes later they reached the summit—and snow. They were on the edge of a snowfield that stretched away before them, a snow-covered glacier. Sal set up the theodolite and tried to take measurements but it was hard to stay upright in the ferocious wind. Visibility came and went as cloud swirled around them. One minute they could see distant peaks and the next they couldn't see each other.

Joe was frightened. It was fantastic to see a glacier but they shouldn't be here. Clambering back to the forest would be slow and dangerous, more dangerous every second. "We need to go now," he said. "This minute. Stay close."

Humphrey was shivering.

"Come on!"

Going down the way they'd come up would be very difficult, but not far beyond the mossy crack in the rock, Joe had seen a vast triangular patch on the mountainside. "We'll run down the scree and be at the bottom in no time."

Humphrey looked scared.

"I'll show you," Joe shouted against the wind. "Scree's just lots of little stones. Remember the sand dunes at New Coalhaven? It's the same—you just pretend to be a rabbit and run and jump. Follow me."

Carrot shot out of his pocket and made for the trees.

Joe heard Sal yell, but he and Humph were already on their way. Humphrey started with cautious side-on steps, but he soon got the feel of the leap-and-slide and began hurtling down the slope like Joe, setting off cascades of pebbles.

It was a long way down, but they landed together at the bottom.

"You're a champion, Humph."

Humphrey's eyes were shining. "Let's do it again!"

"Climbing *up* scree's almost impossible."

Carrot flew onto Joe's shoulder and squawked, "One, two. One missing."

Humphrey clutched Joe's hand, "Where's Sal?"

"She'll be coming."

They listened for the rattle of stones and excited yelps, but there was silence. The slope was fast disappearing under thick rolling cloud.

Joe shouted, "Sa-al!" His shout echoed off the mountain, but when it stopped, they could hear nothing but wind.

Chapter Twenty-One

Never, Ever, Ever Again

Sal was furious. How could those stupid, selfish boys have set off like that, without considering her towing the altimeter? If she went leaping and skidding, the altimeter would unbalance her in an instant. She'd go careering down and end up at the bottom with no skin left on her body. But if she stayed here, she'd die of exposure. Could she carry the altimeter? No, she needed both arms for balance when scree-running.

Cloud swirled around her and the world disappeared. She was done for. But then it lifted for a moment, and she saw the top of the scree again. What if she left the altimeter behind? But it was Ma and Pa's invention. It was their most precious thing, and she was supposed to look after it.

You can do it. It was Pa's voice in her head. *Deep breath. Just think.* She swiped off the tears that were almost ice on her cheeks. It was the cylinder that was precious, not the rest. Maybe she could take it apart. She unscrewed the wheel, then tried to unscrew the cylinder from the shaft with clumsy frozen fingers.

It loosened but wouldn't slide around the bend in the shaft.

"If I don't die here, I want the world to know that this is my last expedition," she shouted at the wind. "I am never ever going to be stuck alone up a mountain again."

One last possibility. She laid the shaft across two rocks and jumped on it with all her force. It snapped! The cylinder slid off the broken end. She fitted it into her rucksack, strapped the wheel to the outside and tucked the broken shaft, yoke and poles between rocks. "Sorry, mountain," she said through teeth clenched with cold.

The important parts were safe. Now she could go. She could only see two metres ahead, and nothing behind, but she could make out the start of Joe and Humph's tracks.

"Never, ever going to climb a mountain again."

She took a giant step onto the scree and started to run. Too fast. She toppled over and tumbled some way before stopping. Grazed hands, sore knees (again), but nothing broken. She got to her feet. "Never, ever, ever."

She licked the blood off her hands and set off again, more slowly. Down and down. She called to the boys but heard nothing.

When she finally got to the bottom of the scree she yelled and yelled, but there was no answering call. She wasn't even sure where she was; she'd long since lost sight of their tracks. She sat on a rock. It began to sleet. Hard icy pellets. Her hands and ears were freezing, and the cloud round her was thickening, if that was possible. She glimpsed trees below but then they disappeared, and she was alone in a grey, featureless world. She could only just see her hand at the end of her arm. Her nose was running; she sniffed—her eyes were running too. She might as well be underwater, it was so wet. She'd probably get hypothermia and die, then Joe would be sorry.

"Sa-al?" Was that the wind or Joe's voice? "Sa-al?"

"Joe?" Sal yelled. "Humph? Joe?" Her voice was muffled and seemed to swirl around her. She scrambled to her feet and shuffled cautiously forwards.

"Sa-al?"

No, that was behind her now. Which way to go?

The voice seemed to come from above and below, and left and right, as though malevolent mountain spirits were mocking her, calling her name from every direction. Shapes like people with outstretched fingers appeared and disappeared into the mist. They were coming to get her.

She was shivering uncontrollably, but also sweating. She couldn't breathe, the cloud was choking her. No air. She was turning into fog—it had swallowed her whole. She was dying. A bigger shape moved in the mist and she tried to scream. The shape disappeared and reappeared, much closer.

Joe.

"We found you! Where've you been?"

Sal couldn't say a thing; she crumpled into a heap on the ground.

Joe and Humph made her sit up and put her head between her knees. They rubbed her hands, made her sip water, then hauled her to her feet. Her panic subsided; she wasn't dead. She wasn't frozen either—yet.

Humph grabbed her hand and clung on. "We were looking

and looking, and shouting and shouting." He was tied to Joe's rope and he insisted on tying Sal in too so they couldn't lose her again.

Joe said that the forest was close. Sal thought she could keep walking. Under the trees, the wind wasn't as fierce, and rain didn't batter their necks.

"Sal?"

Sal grunted.

"I'm really sorry. I forgot about the altimeter."

"I thought I was going to die," Sal whispered.

"You might have," said Joe. "I'm glad you didn't."

"Me too."

Sal kept putting one foot in front of the other and Joe walked behind her, with Humphrey between them. Joe checked his compass and told her which way to go, until at last they found themselves on the path to Bereff Stonch. By the time they squelched across the grass and into the old farmhouse it was dark as night, even though it was only mid-afternoon. The sky was tipping out heavier rain than Sal had thought possible and they were as wet as if they'd been swimming. Their feet, hands and ears were freezing.

But inside, it was cosy. The fire was roaring in the stove and the oil lamp shone warmly. Francie found towels and, although she was ready to collapse, Sal forced herself to change out of her sodden clothes, which Francie and Joe wrung out and hung on the rack above the stove. Hessa handed out a drink called cocol, which made Sal feel warm inside, all the way to her fingers and toes. Then Francie and Joe wrung out all their wet clothes and arranged them on the rack above the stove. Hessa cooked a pile of hot cakes called pikers. She spread them with butter, and the wild berry jam she'd found in the cupboard, and put the chimlacanda and potatoes to bake in the oven.

Sal thought how magical hot food was after a day exploring. It was ten times tastier than normal—and made every tired, achy part of you feel better. When she'd eaten six pikers, she had enough energy to admire the way Francie had filled in the map.

Francie had also drawn a picture. It showed a valley of lying-down trees and part of a building and some kind of tower. She drew a dot on the map and indicated that this was where the scene in the picture was. She drew another picture, of the five of them on a slope looking into the distance. Joe was looking through his telescope.

Sal leaned in. "You saw something strange? You think we should have a look on the way back?"

Francie nodded.

"We will then." Sal took the scroll of paper from inside the altimeter to check heights. They'd descended over two hundred metres on the fan of scree.

"Only two! That's not a lot." Humph sounded disappointed. "I'm five."

"Over two hundred. That's more than a lot, it's humungous," said Sal.

"Oh," said Humph. "Good."

Sal studied the altimeter roll. "Cruxcia is so high. We rose nearly two thousand metres above sea level in the dirigible, then we climbed further yesterday. That's how come there's a glacier so close to a desert." She put the roll back in the altimeter and the maps back in the tube.

Francie was standing by the front door and staring at its frame. She beckoned Sal over. She was smiling but looking unsure.

She'd found a series of marks on the wood, with initials and ages. Years ago, somebody had recorded their children's heights. The initials that appeared most often were CGS and WBS. It showed they were similar heights at ages three and ten, but by fifteen, WBS had shot up to be nine centimetres taller than CGS. Those marks were in faded blue ink. Then there was a set in black ink. WBS was a tall adult aged thirty-nine, and there was a new set of initials that appeared only once. LJS: 11 years 5 months.

Sal suddenly felt shivery. "I've got the funniest feeling. It's a bit like I've dreamed this before. Do you feel the same?"

Francie nodded. LJS: 11 years 5 months. LJS was Leopold Joseph Santander. A wave of realisation washed over Sal. "Hessa, what's your grandmother Clarrie's full name?"

Hessa thought. "She's Clarrie Galina Berris."

"If it was 'Santander' before she married, I think we're related! See these initials?" Joe and Hessa came closer. "LJS is our father. Wilf, your grandmother's twin, was our grandfather, WBS. Pa's father. He died before we were born. Francie worked it out."

"That snowfield today—the glacier!" Joe exclaimed. "Pa went up there when he visited his grandparents' farm, this farm, when he was eleven. You remember, Humph? I told you that story on the Race. When Pa saw the Silver Wolf."

"And Pa made a wish," said Humphrey.

Francie was beaming and nodding with her hands as well as her head.

"Yes! Of course, yes!" Sal's head was fizzing. "Grandpa Wilf went to live far away from his family when he grew up—"

"He did! Grandma Clarrie told me," said Hessa.

"But Pa met his grandparents and aunt once, because when he was eleven, his parents took him to visit. Here's the evidence." It really could be true.

"Vivi called Lysander by all his names when she was cross with him in the quarry. One of them was Santander," said Joe.

"Cousins!" Hessa's eyes gleamed.

"I thought we didn't have any relations at all," said Sal. "But it looks as though…"

Humphrey prodded Hessa. "Are you my cousin for really?"

"We think so! And Vivi, and Lysander, and Lysander's sisters. And their children."

"I got cousins!" Humphrey flung his arms around Hessa's middle.

Hessa started a wild dance around the table with Humph, and Francie joined her. They twirled holding hands, and they stamped and spun. Hessa did a crazy yodel, and Francie answered with a shepherd's whistle. Sal snatched up a saucepan and banged it with a spoon; Humph grabbed Sal's waist, Joe held onto Humph, Francie grabbed Joe, and Hessa held onto Francie and they danced in a line, kicking their legs up together and singing to the beat of the saucepan drum. Carrot perched on the back of a chair and joined in, screeching.

Hessa beamed at them all. "Grandma Clarrie will kiss you to

bits, she'll be so excited. She told me once that she still talks to Wilf every day."

"That's so sad." Sal flopped into a chair. "I wonder if it's why Pa took the job here. A chance to come back to his father's home. Maybe to see if there was any family still here."

"I wonder if Ma knows," said Joe.

"What *I* wonder is, can we eat that chim-a-cana-dinner now?" said Humph.

Hessa took it out of the oven, perfectly cooked. She put a large slice, and a potato, on each plate. They ate in hungry silence. Outside, wind rattled the door, the house creaked, and rain thrashed the roof.

"Best dinner ever, ever," said Joe, and Sal didn't say "you always say that", because she agreed with him.

"Did your father really see the Silver Wolf?" asked Hessa.

Sal told her the story of Pa's visit to his grandparents' farm. He'd never been in mountains before and he badly wanted to touch snow. One day he walked up through the forest and over a sea of rocks, up and up until he finally got there, but it wasn't soft snowman snow. He was right under the snout of a glacier. He broke off an icicle to suck on because he was thirsty. Then he looked out across all the mountains, and decided to be an explorer when he grew up, and see more of the world.

"But climbing had taken most of the day, and it was dark when he reached the forest. He went slowly, feeling his way. Then he started to have a creepy feeling that he was being followed.

"Suddenly a huge monster knocked him over. He was terrified, but he saw that it had saved his life—Pa had been about to step over a cliff. It was a wolf, and it led him down safely to the path to his grandparents' house. They told him that everyone knew of the Silver Wolf, but no living person had ever seen it—and if you saw it, your heart's desire would come true," finished Sal.

"And his heart's 'sire did come true," said Humphrey. "He is an explorer and he's seen lots of world."

"Wow!" said Hessa.

"Hey, Hessa? Why's it raining inside?" Humphrey pointed to a puddle on the floor.

Rain was dripping through the ceiling in several places. Hessa and Humphrey found a bucket and bowls to put under the drips, and Francie followed them with a mop, though she mostly drew patterns on the floor with it. Luckily, the leaks were well away from the bunks and they collapsed, exhausted, into their dry sleeping bags.

Joe started to tell Humphrey a story. It began, "Once upon a time there was a very tired dragon," but then they both fell asleep.

Chapter Twenty-Two

Which Way?

In the middle of the night, Humphrey woke Joe. The candle had burned right out and the room was completely dark. Outside, the storm was still raging. Humph was crying. "I need a pee." He was standing next to Joe. "I'm all wet."

Joe struggled to understand. "Just take your wet pants off, we'll sort it out in the morning," he mumbled.

"I can't!" Humph wailed. "It's all too wet."

"Too wet for what?" Joe groaned.

"Too wet for my feet."

Joe reached for the candle and matches that he'd left on the floor by his bunk, but he felt only water. "Wake up, wake up quick. There's a flood!"

Everyone got out of bed and found themselves stepping into freezing ankle-deep water. Carrot didn't help by flying round the room shrieking. Eventually, Sal managed to light the lantern. Francie caught Carrot and soothed her. Joe rolled his trouser legs up and helped Humphrey. "Good thing you needed a pee,

Humph. This isn't a roof leak; I think the river's trying to get in under the door."

"Boots!" shouted Sal. "Get your boots on quick before they float away. Hessa, grab the food, whatever there is, and put it in your bag. Humph, climb on the bunk and stay there."

Francie helped Sal shove sleeping bags into rucksacks, and their clothes from the drying rack. Joe rescued the water flask that had floated under the table, put the theodolite in his rucksack, strapped the tripod on top and found his rope. He took the lantern and stuck his head out of the door. It was dark outside and the light didn't reach far. All he could see was water, which was nearly up to his knees. The river was trying to take over the hut.

Humphrey was sucking his thumb. "Are we going to climb on the roof, like the story?"

"No roof," said Hessa. "If we go now, we can shelter in the trees up the hill."

Sal stuffed Humph's arms into his jacket. "We'll tie ourselves together."

Joe couldn't help saying, "*Tie*, with the stupid rope, do you mean?"

Francie pulled the waterproof sleeve over the map tube and pushed it as far into her rucksack as she could. They snatched up whatever they saw—a floating sock, a knife, a candle and a dry box of matches from the mantelpiece. Hessa brought Magnus out of the back room, took him to the door and told him to wait for her in a tree. Carrot perched, quivering, on Sal's shoulder.

Joe took the lantern, and an old walking stick to prod the

ground before each step. Humphrey came next, then Francie, with both hands free in order to hang on to Humphrey, then Hessa, then Sal at the back.

Joe stood at the door when they were all tied together. "Ready?" he shouted over the roar of the wind and rain. "It's now or swim."

He opened the door and freezing floodwater swirled into the house, up to the hem of Humph's jacket. They leaned into the current as they organised themselves to follow the swinging light of the lantern.

"Don't pull on the rope. Step. Step. Step," shouted Joe.

In no time their hair was stuck to their heads, their jackets hung cold and heavy, and legs and feet were numb.

Hessa shouted above the wind, "We're a ten-legged sea monster with a light on our head. We're crossing the ocean. What do we eat, Cousin Humphrey?"

"Seaweed," said Humph. "And sea pie, and sea biscuits."

A dark shape rushed through the lantern light straight at Joe. He stumbled back out of its path. It was sleek, black, long and spiky. Something banged his shin under the water, and he yelled, then it was gone. The others huddled up to him.

"Are you all right?" asked Hessa.

"It whacked my shin."

"What was that?" said Sal.

"Either a small tree or an angry mountain shark," said Joe.

He had something else to panic about now, though. He had no idea which way they were facing. When he held the lantern up, the churning black water looked the same in every direction.

Where was the house? Which way had they been going? They needed to head away from the river, but the river was everywhere.

Joe's compass, he realised, was in the bottom of his rucksack. He closed his eyes and listened, but the wind, rain and water noises were coming from every direction. He reminded himself that he was a route-finder. He had to trust himself.

"Joe—hurry! Keep going," Sal shouted, but he ignored her and let his feet shuffle round a bit. Now he was facing north, he was sure. He could see the valley in his mind's eye. The house was back that way, the riverbed to the right; they wanted to leave the river—to go west-north-west. He opened his eyes, turned ninety degrees to the left and led his sea-monster into the darkness.

Sal shouted, "Are you sure this is right?" and "This feels like the wrong way," but he shut his ears and told himself to trust his instinct.

He kept going. The water was deep, up to his waist now. Any deeper and Humph wouldn't be able to stand. Maybe he was leading them straight into the river to drown.

Just as he was deciding that he'd made a mistake and they'd have to turn around, he got tangled in a half-submerged bush. He gingerly felt out each step before trusting his weight, while his arms shoved the bushes aside. The others followed. Bit by bit, the ground rose, and soon they were stumbling up onto the squelchy mud between tree roots. They clambered a few metres higher, into a clearing, and collapsed onto the grass.

"That was scary," said Joe.

Francie squeezed his hand and Humphrey hugged him.

"That was well done," said Hessa.

"And thank goodness you brought the rope, Joe," said Sal. "Sorry about before."

They untied each other with frozen fingers.

"Is there any shelter anywhere? A shed or something?" Joe asked Hessa.

"Hold the lantern up a minute?"

He held it as high as he could. They could see that the clearing was actually part of a path.

"This way." Hessa took the lantern and they followed the light.

Before long she left the path and pushed through some bushes. They found themselves under an enormous umbrella pine with branches that touched the ground around them.

"I used to play houses here, when we came up to check on the sheep."

The ground under the tree was almost dry in places, and sitting down they were out of the wind. They pulled off their waterlogged boots and jackets and dried themselves as best they could. Joe's shin wasn't bleeding but it was sore. Nothing to be done. They shared out the driest socks and wriggled into their sleeping bags.

"What have we got to eat?" asked Joe. They could do with something hot and tasty.

Hessa tipped out her bag. "Dried apples, nuts and—ta-da!" She waved a packet of sweet biscuits. "They were actually a treat for the walk home, but I think we need them now."

Humphrey bit into his biscuit and hummed happily. "Beckett never found biscuits in his rucksack."

They made a caterpillar-cuddle in their sleeping bags, lying close for warmth. Joe must have slept a bit because he woke to find that the wind had died right down. The rain had stopped too, but drips were falling onto his face. He pulled his sleeping bag over his head and dozed off again.

In the morning, the Afa was no longer a river, but a lake. Water flowed briskly around the trees and bushes growing out of it; branches floated past and ducks paddled happily.

The house was gone.

Chapter Twenty-Three

Tired, Cold, Hungry and Sore

Magnus swooped down to Hessa as they skirted the lake, which was already receding. Humph spotted the remains of the house first. It had been swept to the end of the meadow and smashed against solid old fir trees. The sides had fallen out and the roof had folded down; it had flattened into nothing but a pile of old timbers.

Hessa sobbed. Humphrey took her hand and led her in a solemn circuit around the ruins. He picked up a teaspoon and gave it to her. Sal stared at the heap of splintered wood that yesterday had been walls and a floor. She was shaken to realise the power of the water, crumpling what had seemed so solid.

"Our evidence of cousin-ness all gone," said Joe.

"There's the doorframe, though," said Sal. "Let's try to rescue it."

They wrenched out some loose planks to use as levers.

"It's like pick-up-sticks," said Joe.

"Mind the rusty nails. You don't want to get lockjaw," said Hessa.

They worked their planks in under the beam that lay over the door, and jiggled and rocked it until it slid off with a crunch. The door in its frame had detached from the wall.

"We need to lift one side high enough to turn the door over." Joe rolled a rock into the gap when the others jammed their levers in.

"Five more minutes, then we ought to get moving," said Sal. They wedged their planks in again. They were making progress; they kept levering.

Sal forgot her five-minute ruling. "One, two, three—push. Look out!"

They jumped away as the door crashed back down. They hadn't turned it over, but as it fell the frame broke apart. Francie grabbed the upright and Joe helped her pull it clear. They turned it over. There was the plank with the heights marked on it. They soon jemmied it away from the timber it was nailed to.

Francie carried it over her shoulder and they walked on, muddy and scratched but pleased to have saved a bit of Bereff Stonch history.

Usually going home felt quicker than getting there, especially when it was mostly downhill. But not today. Tired and laden with wet gear, they took ages to reach the Jerval turnoff.

Francie indicated they should take the road towards Jerval.

"She showed me last night," Sal explained. "There's something being built, hidden away."

"How far is it?" Hessa asked.

Francie opened two hands three times. Thirty minutes. Each way.

Sal's body ached from yesterday. If only she'd brought Ma's lotions and potions bag, but they hadn't planned being away long enough to justify the weight. Humphrey and Hessa didn't want to walk an extra step, but Francie and Joe were determined.

"You could wait for us here," said Joe. "Or go on home."

Sal had the casting vote. She knew Francie wouldn't have suggested this if it weren't important. "All right, we'll go, but we stick together."

After a few minutes, Francie showed Joe that she wanted him to mark their route; they were about to leave the road. He still had a handful of orange silks in his rucksack, so he tied one to a convenient branch. They left their rucksacks under it and just took Francie's drawing things and Joe's telescope.

Magnus had been flying ahead. Now he came and perched by the marker.

"Bird. Hello bird," said Carrot, perching a respectful distance below him.

Francie surprised Sal. She'd never been expedition leader before, but she plunged into the forest and led the way. They followed a small stream that made a path through the dense undergrowth, splashing right in it since their boots were already sodden. Low-growing branches snatched and scratched at their faces.

Joe paused now and then to tie a silk to a branch.

"We need your slasher, Joe," said Sal. "I hadn't realised quite how much slashing you did for us on the Race. I'm glad I'm not towing the altimeter."

She boosted Humphrey over some tree roots, then hauled her achy body after him. They came to a marsh and had to wade through mud, then they were beyond the stream, climbing a steep hillside where nothing grew on the rocky ground beneath the trees.

They knew they'd reached the top when the forest flowed away downhill on all sides. Joe tied his last marker and Francie led them over the ridge, into a clearing. They collapsed, panting, in a sweaty row. When Sal had her breath back she looked around. She could see for miles over an ocean of forest, the waves of hills and valleys broken by crests of white. The mountains seemed to go on forever.

Francie pointed into the distance. Sal squinted. What was it? Green, green—there! A long way away. A brown valley amidst all the green.

Joe had his telescope out, scanning. "Got it. Lots of chopped-down trees. Something in front. I don't believe it—a dirigible tower. With a dirigible moored, way out in the wilderness."

"What? There can't be."

"See for yourself." He passed the telescope to Sal.

"Holygamoley."

She passed the telescope to Hessa.

"That's wiggity whack. Totally wiggity whack." Hessa was quiet for a minute. "There's something else I can't quite see, but they're buildings, I think. Half-built." She put the telescope down. "I wonder if anyone else knows this is here?"

Humphrey picked up the telescope. "I can see greenness."

"It's so hidden away," said Joe. "Amazing you saw it, Francie."

"But what's it for?" asked Sal, then her hand flew to her mouth. "The new prison—could it be?"

Hessa pulled a face. "But why? It's the middle of nowhere. It rains all the time up here in winter, and it's freezing."

"That might be where those ox carts were going yesterday," said Joe.

The forest was so dense it was impossible to tell from here if there was a track through it.

Francie nodded, opened her pad and sketched the line of carts she'd seen while flying.

"I suppose we should go and find out," said Sal. "But I'm right out of oomph."

"It could take a whole day to get there." Joe was assessing the land with route-finder eyes. "And another day to get back."

"We should head back and tell the others about this as quick as we can," said Hessa.

"Hallowmas Eve is the day after tomorrow," said Sal. "If we can get the prisoners out, then all this doesn't matter."

"Biscuits," said Humphrey. "They're best for oomph."

"Scibits!" said Carrot, swooping down next to Hessa.

"I'd forgotten about them." Hessa felt in her bag.

Humphrey laughed in disbelief. "Nobody forgets about biscuits, silly."

The journey back down the valley took forever. Hessa was quiet and Sal felt as if she were wading through treacle. Her legs slowed right down and her thoughts did too. Her body hurt all over from yesterday's bumps and falls, her feet were sore, and she was just so tired.

On previous expeditions, she'd always felt happy being outdoors, even when she was exhausted. She'd loved the exploring part of the Great Race. This morning, the world was washed and sparkling from the rain, and the views across the valley were beautiful, but she didn't care. Walking in the mountains was not what she wanted to be doing.

She plodded like an automaton down the winding road, past the Max Ext sign and on to the top bridge. The River Afa was higher and faster than yesterday, nearly to the top of the bridge's arches.

Sal looked around. Humphrey was trying to cheer Hessa up: "If you want trees to stop following you, you turn around fast and point your stick and shout 'freeze!'"

"I've decided something," Sal said quietly to Joe and Francie. "This is my last expedition. I'm never doing this again."

Joe stared. "Why? What are you going to do?"

"I'm going to study like Vivi. I'll go to some kind of school. But I'm never going to carry a heavy rucksack and be tired, cold, hungry and sore again."

Now she'd said it out loud, it wasn't just an idea anymore but something that could happen. Francie looked sad. She leaned against Sal and stroked her arm. Carrot landed on her head. "Ever, never, ever."

"Get off, Carrot! Don't worry, Francie. We'll rescue Pa first," said Sal. "I'm not giving up until Pa can go mapmaking again."

Francie rubbed her cheek on Sal's shoulder.

Joe started a walking song. "Tired, cold, hungry and sore. Tired, cold, hungry and sore. Tired, cold, hungry…"

The others joined in and they stomped along together. As Sal sang, her rucksack felt lighter and she had new energy. She was going to be a scholar.

"I know what we need to do," said Hessa. "I'll show you something secret. This way."

They followed her up a track then along a barely visible path.

"Nearly there," said Hessa as they descended towards a stream.

"Is it lunch?" asked Humph-the-hopeful.

Hessa stopped under trees where the stream's banks had been dug out and lined with stones to make a pool. "This is one of the places we come when we're sad or sore or cold. But there's no food here, sorry, Humph."

She put Magnus down on the grass and pinned his jesses to the ground. He stood very still under his hood. Hessa started peeling off her clothes. Sal took off her boots and socks and stuck her foot in the water. It was hot!

Humph took everything off; the others kept their underwear on. The water was glorious, like a bath.

"I've never heard of hot streams," said Joe.

"Thermal," murmured Sal. "This is bliss."

"This is better than even that bath when we finished the Race." Humphrey was perched on a stone with just his head above water. "Betterer even than hot rain."

The others lounged back, beaming at each other through the steam. Sunlight dappled the water and Sal counted at least five different bird calls.

"That one's singing 'din-ner, din-ner'," said Humph. "And that other one said *noodle-coodle-poodle-woodle*."

"You're a noodle poodle," said Joe.

"There are a few secret hot-water pools in the valley," said Hessa. "No visitors allowed."

"We're visitors," said Joe.

"No, you're cousins," said Hessa. "It's totally different."

Sal closed her eyes. "Another minute then we'd better go and tell Vivi what we've found. The new prison. And the sign, which shows the maximum extent of something."

"Maximum extent of mining doesn't sound right," said Hessa.

"Maybe not mining," said Joe. "Maybe Moustache Man wants to chop down the forest."

"All the forest as far as the line." Sal nodded. "Maybe that's the maximum extent of their chopping."

Hessa, Joe and Humphrey started to list all the reasons why chopping down the forest would be terrible. Birds. The Silver Wolf. All the wild creatures. Mushrooms. Nuts. Nothing to make furniture with, or wooden houses. Or paper. Or coffins. And because everyone likes trees.

"Not to mention oxygen," said Hessa.

Sal didn't join in. She was watching the water flowing between rocks. She moved her heel to plug the gap and water flowed over her foot, until she took it away. And then she knew what the line was for. What the GTC was planning to do.

Chapter Twenty-Four

Kleffi and Tage

They rounded a bend in the road and there, ahead, stood several horses on the grass verge. They'd been hobbled: their front legs strapped together to stop them from straying. Their heads hung low and their legs were patched with raw skin where the straps had rubbed. Somewhere up the hill were voices, Cowboy voices, singing and splashing.

"They've found one of our hot pools," said Hessa. "They shouldn't be there."

"This is so cruel. Their legs look really sore," said Sal.

The horses shook their heads and stamped their hind legs in agitation when the children came close. Francie whispered to the nearest one and stroked its nose. It huffed through its nostrils, but stood still and let Sal untie its hobble. It didn't take the children long to free them all.

"We should take them—ride home," said Joe quietly.

"Ooh yes, I never rode a horse, only a donkey," said Humphrey.

Hessa shook her head. "That would be stealing."

"I know," said Joe.

"But letting them go is kindness to animals," said Sal.

They agreed and with a bit of encouragement the horses set off in different directions.

"I hope the Cowboys have a nice long bath, and some of the horses get to Jerval," said Sal. "We'd better hurry, though, in case they don't."

The road was dry; it hadn't even rained here, and a few minutes later they noticed a cloud of dust behind them, heading their way. A horse and trap drew up and the woman called out to Hessa.

"She's on her way to town, she'll give us a ride home."

They climbed up. Hessa sat beside the driver with Magnus while the Santanders squashed into the seat behind with their rucksacks and the plank. Sal watched as the woman talked urgently to Hessa. She looked angry and Hessa seemed shocked, but Sal couldn't hear their words above the clatter of wheels.

They scrambled down at the corner by the haystack and called, "Dasa. Thank you."

"Bad news," said Hessa. "Mundle just announced that the Land Court will be held the day after tomorrow—two days early, and on Hallowmas Eve! Everything's happening at once."

But inside the house, there was also good news: the pantry was full of food just waiting to be eaten.

"Our lovely neighbours are sure we can't manage without Tash," said Hessa.

They'd left three cakes, a basket of doughnuts called kleffi, a tin of cheesy pastries, a pot of soup and two dinners, as well as a big chicken tage, which Hessa put on the fire to heat up.

"That's all from neighbours?" said Joe. He tried to remember if he'd ever known any neighbours. They'd been missing out.

Vivi wasn't there. A note said she'd gone to talk to Stracky's mother. Hessa passed round the pastries and wrote a pigeon message to Lysander, telling him they were home and had lots to tell him. There was also a message from Ma, saying she was well enough to get out of bed. Francie replied, drawing two tiny pictures that showed Sal, Joe, Francie, Hessa and Humphrey climbing up a mountain then coming down again.

Joe watched Francie send the message—she was an expert pigeon handler now—then he went looking for Humphrey, who'd gone worryingly quiet. He found him lying in the hammock on the roof, eating his way through the basket of kleffi. Hercules the cat lay on top of him. Humph's face was covered in sugar.

"I said. I said I was going to die of starvy-ness." Humph didn't even look guilty.

Vivi arrived back and couldn't believe how good the map was. "How did you do that? It's brilliant! Better than anything I imagined."

Hessa hung the lantern over the outside table and put the steaming pot in the middle. They all leaned in as she ladled chicken and dumpling stew into bowls.

"It smells so good," said Hessa, "and we have lots to report, Vivi, but we're actually true-life starving. We've only eaten two biscuits and a cheese pastry since yesterday. All sorts of crazy things have happened, but if we don't eat first we'll die. Can you tell us about the judge while we eat?"

The tage was boiling hot. Joe was so eager he burned his tongue.

"You know they've changed the date. Everyone thinks the GTC did it to mess up our presentation." Vivi scooped up a dumpling. "A Custodian brought me a notice this morning: 'Owing to circumstances beyond our control', is how they put it."

"They can't just change the rules like that," said Hessa. "It's cheating."

"Some adults are liars and cheaters," said Joe. "It was like that on the Great Race, too."

Lysander arrived before they'd finished. He looked in the pot and went to get a bowl.

Humphrey moved along to make room. "Hello Pirate Dander," he murmured.

Lysander ruffled Humphrey's hair. "Ahoy there, me hearty."

Vivi pushed away her plate. "Now tell us. What did you see?"

Hessa put down her fork. "A dreadful flood, which is tragic and nearly drowned us, and we'll tell you about it, but Francie found something even more awful."

They first explained to Lysander about Francie flying—he startled her by kissing her hand and saying that was the best thing he'd heard all year.

"Francie was sure she'd seen something strange, so she took us up a hill to see it," said Sal.

"We think it's where they'll be moving the prisoners," said Joe. "It's high in the mountains."

"You'd never know it was there without a telescope," said Sal.

"It's in the middle of the forest," said Joe. "Tucked away. There are half-built buildings, like skeletons, and a dirigible tower."

Francie showed her drawing.

"Why take them there, of all places?" said Lysander.

Hessa started gathering up the plates.

"They might make the prisoners finish the buildings, then do whatever the GTC's planning next. Free labour," said Sal.

"We've got to get them out!" Hessa's hands shook so hard, the spoons slid off the bowls onto the ground. "Taliesin will die if he has to spend a winter in the mountains, won't he, Vivi? It's freezing and always wet up there, and it snows. He's had pneumonia before, and he nearly died."

Joe was glad Humphrey had wandered off and didn't see Hessa's fear.

"Taliesin, Tash, Kestor ... Kerala," Vivi murmured the names.

"Pa," said Joe.

Hessa was close to tears. "We must get them out!"

At that moment Humphrey came slowly out of the house, carrying a large apple cake with great solemnity. He put the plate reverently on the table. "I choosed which one because you were all doing too much talking."

"Excellent choosing." Vivi cut the cake and handed it round.

"Thanks, Humph. Good cake," said Joe.

"Only two days," said Sal. "The map's done; how about the plan? What's next?"

"First thing tomorrow, volunteers are coming to put names on the map. Francie will draw more pictures and we'll prepare the best, most convincing presentation the Land Court judge has ever heard. He or she will say—" Vivi sat very straight, pulled the back of her shirt over her head like a judge's wig and said in a solemn voice: "'Just because Cruxcians don't have ownership papers for their land doesn't mean anyone else can grab it. The Afa valley is loved by its caretakers and it produces food for everyone.' Then he'll say, 'Governor Mundle, you are not worthy to govern Cruxcia. Leave, before I have you arrested.'"

They all clapped. Lysander cut himself another piece of cake and shoved half of it into his mouth.

"If the judge really did say that, everything would be all right, wouldn't it?" asked Sal. "The only person left in prison would be Mundle."

Lysander nodded. "What a start to Hallowmas!" He sprayed cake crumbs. "I can just see it. And my fireworks extravaganza will celebrate and welcome everyone home. Now, I'd better get back to Grandma. Fare you well."

"Hey, Lysander," Hessa called after him, "one more thing. What was Grandma Clarrie's name before she got married?"

Chapter Twenty-Five

Cousins

Sal held her breath. She hadn't realised how much she wanted this family to also be hers.

"Santander," said Lysander.

"Yes!" said Sal.

"And was her twin's name Wilf?"

"I believe it was."

"Then these Santanders are our cousins!" said Hessa. "They're Wilf's grandchildren."

"Really?" Lysander spun around. "That is beyond excellent. And at Hallowmas too."

"I wondered if they might be. That's brilliant," Vivi laughed. "All of us family! How did you find out?"

Hessa showed Vivi and Lysander the plank from the cottage at Bereff Stonch and explained what it showed. Then she told them about the flood and what had happened to the house.

"We would have drowned, only Humph woke up in time and Joe led us to dry land. I loved that old house." Hessa blew her nose. "Grandma will be really upset, but she'll be happy to know about Wilf's son and grandchildren. Our cousins! Please don't tell her, Lysander. I want to show her the plank and surprise her."

"I won't." He took Sal's hand and touched their joined fingers to his forehead, then to hers. He walked round the table and did the same with Joe and Humphrey. Francie leaned away and Lysander seemed to understand, just smiled at her. "Cousin Sal, cousin Joe, cousin Francie, cousin Humphrey, welcome. See you all tomorrow."

Lysander disappeared through the gate.

Humphrey watched him go. "Night-night, Pirate Cousin Dander," he said softly.

Hessa jumped up. "Let's add you onto our scroll."

Vivi passed Francie a pen. She added Ma and Pa's names neatly below Wilf's, and their own names and birth dates below them. Sal watched Francie's fingers trace back through the generations. Francie understood, so did Joe. Humphrey was the only one who hadn't yet felt the need for more family.

"It's a bit like a map of a river," said Sal. "All the people who have contributed to make us are like the tributaries that flow together to make a river."

Francie smiled and shook her head. She pointed to the top name on the scroll.

"Francie thinks maybe the river flows the other way," said Joe. "We're tributaries flowing back to that first person. What's her name? Endoloya Artenjay."

"So many names, so many stories to get to know," said Sal.

"Maybe in a hundred years someone will point to your name,

Vivi, and they'll say, 'That person helped save Cruxcia when she was only eighteen,'" said Hessa.

Vivi laughed and pretended to flick her with the tea towel.

Humphrey was falling asleep where he sat, so Sal put him to bed. They stoked up the fire and pulled the benches close.

Hessa made them all a mug of cocol. "Tash said for special occasions only. This is a very special occasion."

Sal couldn't wait another minute. "Can we still organise the prison escape in time?"

"That's why I went to talk to Ronia," said Vivi. "We think the best time for the escape will be on Hallowmas Eve. The noise and lights of the fireworks could disguise any escape noises."

Sal thought about that. "That's true. And it gives us the most time."

"And the warders might all go off to see the show," said Hessa.

"The plan's coming together. Stracky and Ronia have taken charge of getting prisoners over the wall. They've worked out how we'll do it. And there's a plan for the dogs. Not killing them," Vivi added quickly, seeing Hessa's face. "We've got someone in charge of the locks, and volunteers to do the actual rescuing."

It was happening! Sal felt overwhelmed with relief.

"Is there anything we can do?" asked Joe.

"The map and notes about the prison have made the plan possible. The next job is less interesting, but important. On the sofa inside there's a bolt of red cloth to be cut into thousands of strips for armbands," said Vivi. "We'll start in the morning."

They were so tired, they were ready for bed after the cocol. But when Sal had cleaned her teeth she went to find Vivi, who was in the scullery washing up. "I think I've worked out what the GTC want to do," said Sal. "Only I can't quite fit the puzzle together. I'd like to tell you first, in case I'm wrong."

Vivi swung her chair round. "Tell me."

Chapter Twenty-Six

Paint and Pyrotechnics Workshop

It was late in the morning when Joe woke.

Humphrey was impatient but waited while Joe ate his farron.

Hessa waved a piece of paper. "I've found Tash's list of urgent jobs. It was in the tea caddy. All we have to do is *pickle the cucumbers, clean the henhouse, store pumpkins in cellar* (Francie and I have just done that). *Dry the corn, pick up windfall apples—make fruit leather. Pick all the beans* (we've done that too), *make chutney* (and that!), *make sauce with the rest of tomatoes, move henhouse to where the beans were and spread the compost.* Why did they have to arrest Tash in the middle of harvest time?"

"Can't you just leave it?" asked Joe.

"We'd starve before next summer," said Hessa. "But we've made a good start and it's great to have your help. Right now, me and Humph are going to meet Lysander at the paint workshop if you and Francie want to come. Then we're going to Mina Mendalwar to pay our respects to the ancestors. Lysander has to come with us or he'll be in trouble with Auntie Pi and Nomie. She's Auntie Pi's partner. She's lovely but she gets cross when anyone isn't properly respectful to the ancestors."

Sal and Vivi had gone to Stracky's house to meet the volunteers labelling Francie's map. There were red strips all over the table.

"I cut some," said Humphrey. "Hessa let me use her specially sharp scissors."

Francie, Joe and Humphrey set off for the paint studio with Hessa, who was carrying a broom and a hearth brush to clean the graves. Stracky drove past going the other way, and called out, "Whisper-chain message. *A dirigible has landed. Twenty workmen lugging tools to the camp.*"

"I will not panic," said Hessa, but she looked worried. Before they reached the studio, she called in at two houses to pass the message on. "Stracky's our link, then we're their link. That's how the whisper-chain works."

When Hessa unlocked the studio door, Francie stood in astonished silence. Joe could feel her quivering. The room was like an artist's palette. Paint had been blobbed and daubed over the walls. Splodges of carmine red sat on midnight blue, which was run through with streaks of lemon. The floor had received the same treatment and colourful footprints tracked across it. There were no windows, but a band of translucent material at the top of the walls let in light and made the ceiling appear to float.

Although the walls and floor were a chaos of colour, everything in the centre of the room was orderly. Pots of brushes and trays of pens were laid out neatly on a great circular table. Around the table, shelves held boxes of pencils, tubs of chalk, tins of pastels, baskets of crayons and racks of inks, tubes, jars and bricks of paint. Francie spun and danced from wall to wall and shelf to shelf, touching her fingertips to everything.

Humph put his hands on his hips and looked around. "I think you love this house, Francie. I think you want to marry it and live here forever."

Francie jiggled, clapping and grinning, then Lysander arrived with some younger children and she backed away into a corner.

"Greetings, cousins. Greetings." He bounded over to a stack of bins, unclipped the lids and poured powder into the buckets the children were carrying.

Hessa wrote down what he was taking. "Half a bucket each of *spring blue*, *flame*, *persimmon*, *snow* and *apple*." Plumes of coloured dust rose and drifted together above their heads: orange and purple and turquoise. Francie was transfixed.

"Also, I need big paper," said Lysander.

The paper was hanging in piles of different sizes over the bars of a giant clothes horse. Lysander pulled down a couple of sheets and rolled them up. Joe and Francie stared. Who knew that paper was even made that big?

"Vivi wants paper, too. Let's take lots to be safe." Hessa pulled down several sizes. Francie rolled them up and stroked the roll against her cheek. They followed Lysander and the buckets of colour to the pyrotechnic workshop across the yard. Outside its big open doors, a boy called Idris was experimenting with sound, rolling a mop inside a metal drum to make an eerie noise, then scraping the drum with a metal bar, while another boy listened and decided which noise was best.

"Madoc is in charge of the sound effects," said Hessa.

As they went inside, Joe told Humphrey, "No touching anything in case it explodes. Promise?" Humphrey pressed his hands into his armpits.

The workshop was full of children and Lysander introduced them all. Lilja and Max were funnelling coloured powder into cardboard tubes; the bucket-carriers lined up the buckets under their workbench. A circle of younger ones sat on the floor making paper flowers and threading them into garlands, with help from Hessa's friend Etta. Some older children were weighing chemicals into jars and labelling them, and a girl crouched on the floor was wiring fireworks together.

Lysander said, "It's going to be the best show ever. We have music, ghost children, clouds, smoke, mirrors—everything."

"Do you want to take anything over to the Mina?" asked Hessa. "We're going there now, and you're coming with us to explain to the ancestors. You'll be in big trouble with Auntie Pi and Grandma Clarrie if you don't."

"I'm coming, I'm coming!" said Lysander. "Stracky's taking the big stuff later, but we'll hide some special effects around there now."

He checked that the other children knew what to get on with, then loaded Humphrey, Joe and Francie with garlands and Hessa with some brushes. He packed the special effects into two bags, with more garlands on top to hide them.

Humphrey trotted beside Lysander. "What's ancestors?" he asked.

"Old dead family. People like your father's great-grandfather."

"Where are they? Can we see them?"

"No. They've been dead for a long time. They're buried in the ground."

"Like treasure. Let's dig them up."

"No digging. We're just going to talk to them."

"What about?"

"I have to warn them that I'm going to let off fireworks all over their hill. The miners have put their tents up where we usually do that."

"You should have told them ages ago. Are you a bit worried about what they might do, Lysander?" Hessa teased.

"What might they do?" As they crossed the bridge, Joe dropped a stone into the river with a satisfying plop.

"They could make it rain tomorrow night," said Hessa. "That would be very mean."

When they reached the Mina, a Custodian blocked their way.

Hessa waved her brushes. "We're visiting the ancestors."

The Custodian nodded reluctantly and let them pass.

"Lots of children have been coming up here, cleaning and decorating family graves for Hallowmas," said Lysander when they were out of earshot. "The Custodians are used to us. Tonight the miners down below might have a few surprises, though—a taste of what's coming tomorrow night."

They were under some of the tallest, laciest trees Joe'd ever seen. Hessa led them to one side of the clearing, where a spring spouted from a rock. She washed her hands and lifted water to her mouth and forehead, then she put her hand on the trunk of a tree. "Greetings to the poet, the parent, the gardener and all my ancestors who came before me and are part of me. We've come to say hello, and to tell you that we're doing our best to make the miners leave, and the GTC. Please support us with your knowledge and experience to get Cruxcia back. Dasa. You go next, Joe."

Joe's mind went blank, but Francie smiled encouragement at him. He wet his hands in the spring, touched his forehead and put one hand on the silvery bark of another towering tree. "Dear ancestors. You've got really beautiful, enormous trees growing round you. From you, I suppose. I think they're so big because they're really old; you probably are too—I know you've been here a long time. I've discovered that some of you are actually my ancestors, not just Hessa's, which I didn't know before. I hope you won't mind if I ask, but we really need to get our Pa and everyone out of prison, so any help you can give would be great. Dasa."

When he'd finished, he looked at the canopy high above. He felt as he did when he looked up at the stars—small, unimportant and safe.

"That was good," said Hessa.

"My turn." Humphrey reached up to wash his hands. "What are we doing again?"

"Sending greetings to our ancestors."

"Oh, yes." He turned around slowly. "Hello 'cestors. You're all buried. I hope you don't mind. Hessa's my cousin. So is Vivi and Pirate Dander. You have very big trees. I like kleffi. And Hercules. Um, I saw a bear once. And please don't make it rain tomorrow. Thank you."

Lysander clapped, which made Humphrey turn pink. "Now Francie."

Francie smiled. She gave the roll of paper to Joe, washed her hands, touched her forehead and a tree, and danced a spinning and swaying message. High in the canopy the leaves quivered and scattered sunlight on her hair and arms.

When she'd finished, the others clapped. Then they left Lysander to talk privately to his ancestors, and followed a path that wound round and round the hill. They swept the moss and leaves away from a group of graves that Hessa said contained their great, great-great and great-great-great-grandparents, and their great-aunts and great-uncles. Joe's skin prickled at the thought of all those people connecting him to the past.

When Francie had decorated their headstones with the garlands of paper flowers, Hessa took them to the oldest legible grave on the Mina. A pattern of green and yellow moss had crept over the worn letters, which read: *Dulcinia Narabon*. Vivi wanted the judge to see it and had asked Francie to draw the ancient stone.

Before they'd finished, Lysander came up the path, scattering pebbles as he went. They were special stones that he said would glow in the dark. Joe helped him hang tubes of different lengths in the trees, which would make ghostly noises as the evening breeze blew through them. Then Lysander unpacked some strips of thin metal, hanging from strings. "These need to go in the trees, too, away from the path. Listen." He shook them gently.

Their low *whurrer-whurrer* immediately made Joe feel on edge and anxious. "It's the sound of worrying," he said.

They hung the worry strips in the trees high above the miners' camp and went back to the pyrotechnic workshop together. Stracky had arrived and was impatient to transport the heavy props for the show up to the Mina. Joe, Francie and Hessa helped load up the cart with two large mirrors wrapped in blankets, two empty metal bins, a shiny metal cone, a mop, beaters, a large sheet of metal hanging from a frame, a brazier, several lanterns, a sack of wood chips, glass flagons full of chemicals, a gong, chimes, a fire drum and many boxes of fireworks.

"I can't wait to see what this is all for," said Joe. "Hurry up, tomorrow night."

When they got back to the kaleidoscope house, there was a Custodian standing outside the gate in the lane. Sal and Vivi were inside, upset and angry.

"They searched the house again," said Vivi.

"It was Loofus and Clocksley," said Sal.

This time the Custodians had thrown cushions off the sofa and bedding off the beds, and pulled clothes out of cupboards and onto the floor.

"They looked in the pigeon loft, up on the roof and in the henhouse. And they killed one of the chickens and just took her," said Sal. She was trying to drink a cup of tea, but her fingers were trembling so hard it kept slopping over. "They didn't look under the workbench in Magnus's shed, though. Ma's carpetbag and the tool bag are still safe."

"They kept asking, 'Where's Angelica Santander?'" said Vivi.

"We said, over and over, 'She's not here, we don't know, we wish we knew, we haven't seen her,'" said Sal. "But they wouldn't listen."

"They said, 'We're watching you,'" said Vivi. "That's scary."

Francie curled up in a corner of the sofa and piled cushions over herself. Humphrey cuddled next to her, spreading a rug over them both.

Joe felt sick. His thoughts weren't working. "Why do they want Ma so badly?"

"Maybe they're just trying to scare us," said Sal, "because they know Vivi's going to make the submission."

Hessa tickled Humphrey out of his hiding place, and when Vivi asked her, Francie emerged to show her the picture of Dulcinia Narabon's headstone.

"It's perfect," said Vivi.

Francie rolled it into the tube with the maps and other pictures. Then they worked together to remake beds, fold away clothes and straighten everything up. Sal and Vivi packed up the papers they'd need in the morning, then Vivi rolled out of the house to tend to Magnus and the pigeons before it got too dark. She sent a message to Lysander telling him they'd appreciate escorts in the morning, in case the Custodians tried to make it difficult for her to get to the Land Court hearing.

Everyone was hungry, but no one wanted to sit out by the fire in the dark yard when there might be Custodians just over the wall, so they stayed inside and ate a neighbour's rice dish cold. Eventually Hessa and Humphrey fell asleep on the sofa. Sal checked through the maps for the final time. Everything was as it should be.

"What about your mother's signature?" Vivi asked. "They might be waiting for you to take the map for her to sign and seal, so they can follow you and arrest her."

"In that case…" Sal pulled the seal and wax from her pocket, "they're going to be very disappointed."

Chapter Twenty-Seven

The Land Court

The whisper-chain had done its work, and in the morning a group of Cruxcians were waiting by the gate to make sure Vivi got safely to the Societies' Meeting Hall where the Land Court was to be held.

The hall was lined with polished wood and had high windows. Sal automatically counted the seats: thirty rows, fifteen each side of the centre aisle, plus a gallery. They sat in the front row: Vivi in Doris, with Hessa next to her, then Sal, then Humphrey, Joe and Francie. Sal tried to breathe deeply. Vivi had asked her to speak and she kept imagining all the seats full of people looking at her. What if no words came out of her mouth?

Stracky was already here, unloading crates and baskets of colourful produce and arranging them along the front of the platform: glossy purple aubergines, shiny red and green chillies, piles of juicy-looking pears, plump knobbly pumpkins and things Sal couldn't identify. "It all comes from valley farms," said Vivi. "The judge needs to see the good things that we grow."

Sal and Humphrey looked at the embroidered banners hanging between the high windows and tried to guess which society each represented. The chimney and mugs must be potters. The needle and thread on a bolt of green cloth would be textile workers. Humph said the coloured bottles were like Auntie Pi's, the apothecary. A pile of books next to a printing press could be paper workers or printers. Or librarians? There were so many societies. She asked Vivi about the scroll with a pen, ink bottle and abacus.

"That one's yours and mine, Sal. It's for studying."

"There's a society for *students*?"

"Of course. For people who spend their days researching, thinking about how things work and how the world could be improved for everyone."

"Oh!" Sal closed her eyes. After the Race, the women from the Association of Women Explorers had told her about college, which had sounded wonderful, and now she let herself imagine being part of a whole society of such people. She felt giddy with possibility.

The hands of the clock above the platform ticked around slowly and the seats filled up. A stream of people came over to Vivi and squeezed her shoulder or touched her hand and muttered encouragement. Sal could hear the people behind her arguing about whether the miners were going to dig for coal or gold. She was tempted to turn round and tell them they were both wrong, but they'd hear soon enough.

A Custodian came through a side door and rang a bell. People shushed each other and the crowd went quiet, then who should enter but Tall and Short, carrying a map tube and box of documents. They swept up the side aisle and took front seats, just across from Vivi. Sal's insides churned and sloshed. She exchanged looks with Joe. What were they doing there? Neither Vivi nor Hessa had any idea. Then the bell rang again and a Custodian called, "All rise for His Honour, Judge Scumble."

Sal had imagined that a Land Court judge would be big and intimidating, but the judge who was helped up the steps onto the platform was old, small and frail. In a curly wig and oversized scarlet robe trimmed with white fur, he looked as if he were playing dress-ups. He sat down and fussed with his papers and spectacles. Finally, he cleared his throat. "Good morning, ladies and gentlemen." His voice was whiskery and quiet. Everyone strained forward to hear.

"Yes. The Land Court is now sitting. We have two presentations to hear today. The first presentation is by, er, Miss Abercrombie and Mr, er, Zander. Yes?"

From all around the hall came the murmur of people asking each other who they were.

Tall and Short went onto the stage, bowed to the judge and stood behind a small table. "Your Honour, I am Clarice Abercrombie," said Tall, "and this is my partner, Norton Zander."

Sal was so surprised to discover, first, that Zander Abercrombie were two people, and, second, that they were the very ones who'd employed Waldo Watkins and Pa, she nearly missed what they had to say.

"We represent, and are agents for, the governor of Cruxcia and the Grania Trading Company." Clarice Abercrombie looked straight at Sal with a sneer. Sal wanted to hide under the seat. "Our submission is brief and straightforward, Your Honour. The land in the Afa valley has traditionally belonged to all the people of Cruxcia. Governor Mundle represents the people of Cruxcia. He intends to develop the valley's resources for the benefit of all.

"We are submitting this map, as required, which shows the River Afa, its tributaries and all the land within its watershed. We ask that you declare these lands to be under the stewardship of the governor, to safeguard them in perpetuity."

"What does perpetuity mean?" Sal whispered to Vivi.

"Forever," Vivi whispered back.

The judge asked to see their map and peered at it closely. "There appear to be no boundaries between farms in this valley," he observed. "Presumably that is because there has never been individual ownership, yes?"

Norton Zander nodded. "Exactly, sir."

"Well, this all seems straightforward and uncontestable," said the judge. "I will stamp my seal on the declaration of stewardship and, um, perhaps that is business concluded for the morning?"

As soon as everyone had heard and understood the judge's words, the hall rippled with shouts and angry muttering.

"One moment please." Vivi propelled Doris around the platform and up the ramp at the side. Sal followed with the box of papers and the map tube. Vivi parked herself on the platform opposite the judge. "Your Honour, you said that you would hear two submissions today and you've only heard one. My name is Vivi Terrabynd and I will now present the second submission."

Joe shouted, "Go Vivi!" Others in the crowd did, too.

The judge glanced at Abercrombie and Zander. "Carry on, Miss Terrabynd."

Tall and Short left the platform and sat down, sniggering quietly together.

Vivi ignored them. "I am presenting this submission on behalf of my family and all the people of the Afa valley and the town of Cruxcia. I'll begin with some background information." She cleared her throat. "This valley feeds everyone who lives in it, as well as the people of Cruxcia town. This display is just a selection of the food we grow in our fields and gardens, which are enclosed by these ancient stone walls."

Sal held up Francie's drawing of one of the high stone walls.

"Objection, Your Honour, but how is this possibly relevant?" asked Short.

The judge looked over his spectacles. "Are you suggesting that old things aren't relevant?"

"No sir, of course not."

The audience laughed as he sank back into his seat, and Sal felt a flicker of hope.

The judge frowned.

Vivi next talked about Mina Mendalwar, where the oldest legible grave belonged to Dulcinia Narabon who had died aged sixty-one and been buried there 479 years ago. Sal held up Francie's drawing. Then Vivi asked Sal for the map of the valley. It was now covered with tiny writing. Sal held it up for everyone to see, then she took it close to the judge, who peered at it. Vivi explained that there *were* boundaries between farms. She asked Ronia to come up and tell the judge about her farm.

Ronia came onto the platform carrying an unwieldy box that she placed at her feet. "I live and farm here." She pointed on the map. "We've farmed this land for at least eight generations and one of my sons will take over when he's old enough. And in here," she heaved the box onto the judge's table, "are documents to prove that."

The judge looked appalled at the box of papers.

"Objection." Short got to his feet. "Your Honour, that's a new submission."

"Oh, yes." The judge shook his head. "No new submissions."

"This is part of *my* submission, sir," said Vivi firmly. "I intend to bring evidence of centuries of unbroken stewardship of all the farms in the valley, and the river banks and forest. Will everyone with evidence please stand up?"

All over the hall people stood, clutching baskets, boxes and rolls of paper. Ronia took her box back to her seat. "These people have brought their farm accounts, letters, diaries and grazing records that have been handed down over the centuries. Torren Bastermole, over there, has a three-hundred-year-old painting of the house he lives in, signed by the artist, his nine-times great-grandmother. Kaliani Matebill has the dress that's been worn by at least six generations of her family on their wedding day, and records to prove that each was married from the same valley farmhouse. We have records showing more than five hundred years of love and care for our land.

"These farms have boundaries, but they are not in any land

register because they have never been bought or sold. We do not sell our land. If there is no one in the family who wants to look after a place, someone else from the valley or town takes over."

She lifted her chin and looked Judge Scumble in the eye. "Your Honour, this land has been in good stewardship for over five hundred years, and is in good stewardship now. The evidence is in the crates of fruit and vegetables in front of you, and in what these people hold. Come out to the valley with us and we'll show you how this land has been and is being cherished, and how it will be cherished in the future."

Vivi was so good—she ought to be a judge, thought Sal.

"It is six years since the GTC decided we needed a governor in Cruxcia and chose Mundle. We were given no choice. The GTC brought armed Custodians, so we couldn't argue. Your Honour, people of Cruxcia, do you know why Mundle now wants the valley to be put in his name?" Sal held up Waldo Watkins' map of the plain. "We believe he is claiming the uncultivated land on the plain beyond the town for himself and the GTC."

Vivi was coming to the moment in the presentation when Sal had to speak. The map shook in her hands. She put it down and gripped Doris's handles to steady herself. Vivi addressed everyone in the hall. "They do not intend to mine for gold or coal in our valley." She paused. "They are planning to drown it, for the water."

There was a moment's pause while her words sank in, then a gasp of horror from the crowd, followed by uproar. The judge banged his gavel hard on the table, until Vivi's voice could be heard again. "My cousin Sal Santander will explain why the miners are here and what they're going to do—unless we stop them in time."

Sal's whole body was fluttering. She kept one hand on Doris. Time stopped. Everyone looked at her. "The GTC plan to build two dams, one each side of Mina Mendalwar," she began.

"Louder," shouted a voice from the back.

She said it again, shouting to the back of the hall. "But how do you build a solid dam when the river you're damming keeps washing your building materials away? The answer is, you move the river first."

Hessa and Joe had come onstage. They held up diagrams to show what Sal meant. Sal felt braver now. Everyone was listening hard. She went on. "That's why the miners are here. They'll dig a tunnel through the bottom of the Mina for the river to flow through while they build the dams either side. Once the dams are built, they'll block the tunnel, and the valley will gradually fill with water, until all the homes and farms in the valley are at the bottom of a great lake."

Sal held up the map with the single contour line. Francie had coloured the new lake in blue.

Vivi continued. "This map shows the extent of the planned lake. It will be eighty metres at its deepest, and you'll see that the expensive mansion the governor has built for himself is now at the water's edge."

There were groans and shouts of derision.

"The GTC and the governor will take all the water they need for their cotton bushes, and make a fortune. I expect they'll sell the rest."

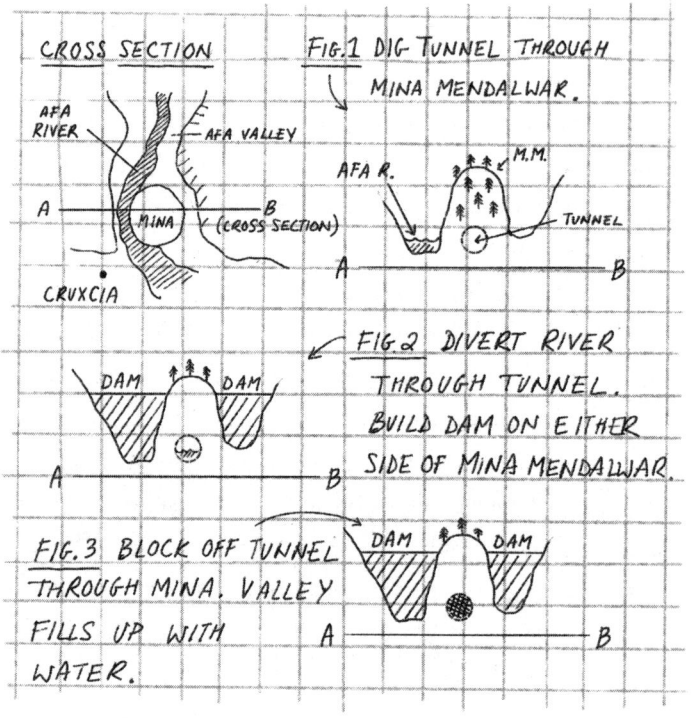

"We'll starve," someone shouted.

"I think the GTC will bring in food by ornithopter for those who can afford it," said Vivi. "Everyone else will have to leave. Live in Porto Pearls."

Sal thought of the families she'd seen sleeping on the street.

"And there's one more thing. Tell them what you saw, Sal."

Sal took a deep breath. "High up in the mountains, there's a valley. A tributary to the River Afa. In this valley, there are buildings and a dirigible tower." She paused to allow the collective gasp to subside.

"I sawed that too," said Humphrey.

Sal continued, "The dirigible tower allows the GTC to bring in workers and materials, we think to build another dam and flood that top valley. They seem to be planning a whole series of dams on the Afa to power machinery and collect water to irrigate the plain."

Vivi said, "It's the prisoners who will be building that dam, and perhaps this one too. Now, a dam in the mountains might be a good idea, I don't know, but it has to be decided by us, for all of us. Nothing to do with Mundle and the GTC, who've been getting rich from us for long enough."

As she spoke, the audience began to stand, more and more of them, until everyone was on their feet. It was strangely terrifying. Everyone in the hall stood in silence, as if waiting for a signal.

Vivi turned to the judge. "We are *not* asking for permission to continue our stewardship of the Afa valley. We are informing you that we will continue to look after this land into the future. We don't need land registration in order to know who looks after what, but apparently *you* do, so on our map you'll find the names of every family who farms in the valley or looks after woodland, forests and river banks on behalf of every Cruxcian."

She held up a wad of paper. "And this is a list of each citizen over the age of ten. There are nineteen thousand, eight hundred and eighty-five of us. Together we claim ownership."

There was a roar of approval. The crowd shouted and cheered and hugged one another. The judge banged his gavel on the table, and banged it again, harder, until eventually there was silence, but everyone stayed on their feet.

Judge Scumble blinked at Vivi with his watery eyes. "Well, that was a thorough submission, young lady. Let me see the map more closely. And I need to check the signature." Sal spread the map of the valley on the table in front of him. He looked at the bottom corner where a red wax seal was fixed over a signature and the words:

ANGELICA SANTANDER

ACCREDITED MEMBER OF THE
INTERNATIONAL SOCIETY OF MAPMAKERS

The judge looked at the silent crowd, then raised his eyebrows at Abercrombie and Zander. He cleared his throat. "This appears to be in order. I will now retire to deliberate. I will give my judgment shortly."

Two Custodians came onto the platform and escorted Judge Scumble out to a back room. There wasn't a sound from the hall until he'd gone. Then Zander and Abercrombie crossed the stage in tight-lipped fury and also went out the back, through a chorus of boos and hisses. Zander was carrying a briefcase.

As soon as they were out of sight, the hullaballoo began. Sal was scared for Vivi, who was swamped by people, cheering, stamping and shouting "Vi-vi, Vi-vi!" But when she caught a glimpse of Vivi through the throng, she was laughing.

Eventually a voice shouted for silence and Doris was wheeled back onto the platform. Lots of people stood up and spoke, saying how proud Vivi's ancestors would be of her. Someone said that Moustache Man owed lots of money. He'd be bound to end up in prison now—he needed that water for his cotton crop.

"What about all the people already in the prison? What about our father?" Sal asked the others.

"The Custodians will have to free everyone now, won't they, Vivi?" asked Hessa, but Vivi was surrounded by too many people to hear.

Lysander came running from the side door and leaped onto the platform. "The judge—he's just got into a carriage and told the driver to take him to his ornithopter, top speed!"

A Custodian strode onto the platform. Lysander jumped over the sacks of potatoes and onions and landed in the crowd. The Custodian shouted for silence and waved a piece of paper. The crowd inside the hall hushed, though there was still a lot of angry noise coming from outside.

"Right. Here it is," he announced. "The Honourable Judge Scumble has reached his decision. His decision is final and no appeal will be entered into." He cleared his throat. "The submission of Vivi Terrabynd is—dismissed. The case has been won by Abercrombie and Zander on behalf of Governor Malvicious Mundle of Cruxcia, on the grounds that—"

No one heard what the grounds were. The courtroom erupted in fury.

Chapter Twenty-Eight

Will This Change Everything?

Joe pulled Humphrey and Francie to the side of the hall as everyone started screaming and shouting at once. They climbed onto seats to see better. Sal and Hessa were clearing a path to the far door for Vivi and Doris to get out. People made way, then surged out after them, and out of the other exits, their faces furious, or distraught. The woman beside Francie burst into tears.

There was such a hubbub, Joe couldn't make out what exactly was being yelled. He held on tight to Humphrey and they followed others through a side door, up a narrow alley and out into the square. They skirted around two Custodians cradling rifles, and around the growing crowd until Joe spotted Sal standing on the plinth of Moustache Man's statue. Francie climbed up beside her and hung onto a bronze arm.

"What's happening?" Joe had to shout above the noise.

"The judge has gone. They say Tall and Short bribed him. He'll be at the Sky Worff by now with a bag of gold—he's probably in the air already."

Joe was astonished. "Did Tall and Short leave, too?"

"No, it seems they went back to Mundle's mansion. Ronia's with Vivi and Hessa—they're trying to calm people."

Those outside the hall had grown even angrier. They seemed to agree on something and moved off in a mass across the square.

There was a shout, a scream—and a shot.

Joe and Sal looked at each other. *Was that what I think it was?* They jumped off the statue and ducked; Sal threw herself over Humphrey. Another shot. Two shots. Everyone was running for cover and screaming. Moments later the square was empty, apart from a little cluster of people in front of the hall and a clump of Custodians watching them from a few paces away.

In the middle of the square lay a wheelchair on its side.

"Vivi!"

Joe and Sal ran. Other were running too. Someone was crying. There was blood on the ground. Lysander was there—he lifted Doris onto her tracks. Stracky and Ronia were helping Vivi up. But the blood wasn't Vivi's, it was Hessa's. She was sitting on the ground, clutching her arm. Blood streamed from her shoulder and trickled off her fingers.

The crowd was forming again, shouting at the Custodians. Lieutenant Loofus waved his curved sword as if preparing to slice up the people pushing forward; two other Custodians pointed pistols, first at Ronia, then at Vivi, then at Joe.

Several other Custodians backed away. One kept muttering,

"He shot a little girl! He shouldn't have done that! He shot a little girl!"

Someone wrapped a blanket around Hessa and lifted her onto Vivi's lap. Vivi held her tight. "Push me. Quick. We need to get her to Auntie Pi."

Joe and Sal took a handle each and Francie held Humphrey's hand.

"This will change everything!" Vivi's shout echoed around the square.

They didn't try to talk, just pushed Doris as fast as they could, following Vivi's directions. "Turn left. Right here. And right by the fountain." Then, "Check they're not following."

Joe checked. They weren't.

Hessa groaned.

"They shot her—with a gun! Will she be all right?" Joe wasn't sure if he'd spoken the words aloud.

"We're here. Bang on the gate."

The gate was like a door in the wall between two tall buildings. It wasn't Auntie Pi's house. There was a bell. Joe pulled it and heard a clang inside. The door was opened by Auntie Pi.

"Thank goodness you're here," said Vivi.

Auntie Pi unwrapped Hessa's blanket, looked at her wound, clucked her tongue and told the Santanders to go and find their mother. This was Nomie's family house, where Nomie and Auntie Pi had brought Ma to be safe from the Custodians.

They found Ma sitting in a tiny garden. She heard them and looked up. She stood up and held out her arms. Francie got to her first for a hug, "Francie! Humphrey!"

Joe hugged her tight. Her hair smelled different—like flowers.

"Wait—" she held them away. "Are you all right? Who's bleeding?"

Joe looked at the others. They all had blood smears on their faces and hands, and bloodstains on their clothes.

"Hessa's hurt." Sal was careful not to say what by. "That's her sister, Vivi."

Vivi sat in Doris by the door, tense and silent, waiting to see how Hessa was. They heard Pi say something to Vivi, then Vivi called, "She's all right. It's not serious, thank the ancestors."

The relief was overwhelming. Francie and Humphrey started crying.

Now they could talk. They sat on a low wall beside Ma and introduced her to Vivi. Pi and Nomie had told Ma what was going on in Cruxcia and about Pa being in prison, but she wanted to know more and kept saying, "I didn't realise this place was so dangerous."

"It's not, it's really not." Sal distracted her by telling her that Francie had flown over the prison and had actually seen Pa, and that he'd smiled at her. Ma hugged Francie and cried with happiness.

None of them mentioned that the prisoners were to be moved tomorrow.

Humphrey poked Ma's knee for attention. "I climbed a mountain and saw a—what did I see, Joe?"

"A glacier."

"I saw a glacier, but I didn't get a nicicle like Pa did with the Silver Wolf. And we got cousins. One of them is Pirate Dander."

Joe and Sal explained to Ma about being related. Ma understood straight away. She laughed and looked as delighted as they felt. "That explains it," she said. "Leo was so keen to take this job, even though he'd turned down other expeditions. I think he desperately wanted to see if his father's family were still here, but he didn't say so because he was afraid that nothing would come of it. Poor Leo."

Then Auntie Pi came out with Hessa. Her left shoulder was bandaged and her left arm strapped to her chest, not because it was broken, but so she couldn't use it, and set the bleeding off again.

"Dasa, ancestors," said Vivi, and Hessa bent down so Vivi could hug her.

Joe wiped his face on his sleeve. "I thought you might die or something. There was so much blood."

"There was, wasn't there? A great puddle of it."

"She was lucky," said Auntie Pi. "The bullet only skimmed through her flesh—no broken bones."

Vivi couldn't stop grinning. "If you're all right, Hessie-Bess, we need to go home, urgently. We've got a lot to do, and only a few hours."

Ma asked what they were busy with and Vivi said, "On top of everything else, it's Hallowmas Eve and we're all involved in the Hallowmas show—one way or another."

"My goodness," said Ma. "Glaciers, family, shows. I thought I'd only been sick a few days."

"And there's more," said Joe. "We'll tell you tomorrow."

Ma looked at them as if she were seeing them through new

glasses. She smiled and nodded and blew kisses as they left. Auntie Pi had said Hessa could walk home if she promised to rest afterwards. They hurried back to the house together, talking all the way.

"Did you notice Ma didn't shriek when Auntie Pi said 'bullet'," said Sal. "I thought she'd have fifty fits and make us stay where she could see us for the rest of our lives."

Joe had noticed. "She trusts us."

"I'm sorry about lying to your mother," said Vivi. "I just didn't want her to worry."

"Well, it's true, we have got a lot to do, and freeing the prisoners is part of the Hallowmas show," said Joe.

"Your presentation was brilliant," said Hessa. "But they were never going to let you win. The GTC say they're doing things for everyone, but by 'everyone' they mean themselves. Greedy cheaters. It's shameful."

"Shameful is exactly what it is," said Vivi. "They have slogans like *Great Times Coming, Growing Together Cruxcia* and *Gateway to a Cornucopia*. But none of that is for Cruxcians."

"I wonder how much they had to pay the judge," said Joe.

Ronia and Stracky were waiting at the house. They were very relieved to see Hessa. "You were as white as my bed sheets," said Ronia. "I don't know how I could have faced your dear mother if you'd been badly hurt."

Ronia had lit the fire, brought fresh bread and heated up one of the neighbours' dinners. Hessa passed Sal the bread knife. "I can't slice bread one-handed."

They dished up, then Ronia said, "What I want to know is, how did you get your mother's signature under the seal?"

Francie smiled and pushed her sketchbook towards Ronia.

"Sign your name," said Joe. "She'll show you." Ronia signed the page, and Francie copied her signature.

"Identical!" said Vivi. "It's a good thing you're such an honest person, Francie."

"They cheated a lot, so we cheated a little," said Sal. "Just this once."

While they finished eating, Ronia told them what she'd heard. "Everyone we trust knows to take a red armband with them tonight. Everyone we trust knows the uprising will happen, but not how it will start, apart from those going over the wall. The whisper-chain is ready. There'll be thousands of people out watching the fireworks and they'll all get the message whispered to hurry to the prison when we need them."

Joe took an apple from the bowl. Carrot flew down and pecked at it.

Sal shook her head. "No, Carrot, off the table."

Carrot looked balefully at Sal, took the stalk in her beak, dragged the apple to the edge of the table and pushed it off. They all laughed.

Everyone got busy. Francie made copies of her prison map for those going over the wall. Ronia took them to distribute, along with all the red strips that Joe and Sal had cut so far. Joe and Sal kept cutting.

Hessa was told to lie in the hammock, which she argued about, but finally did, and almost immediately fell asleep.

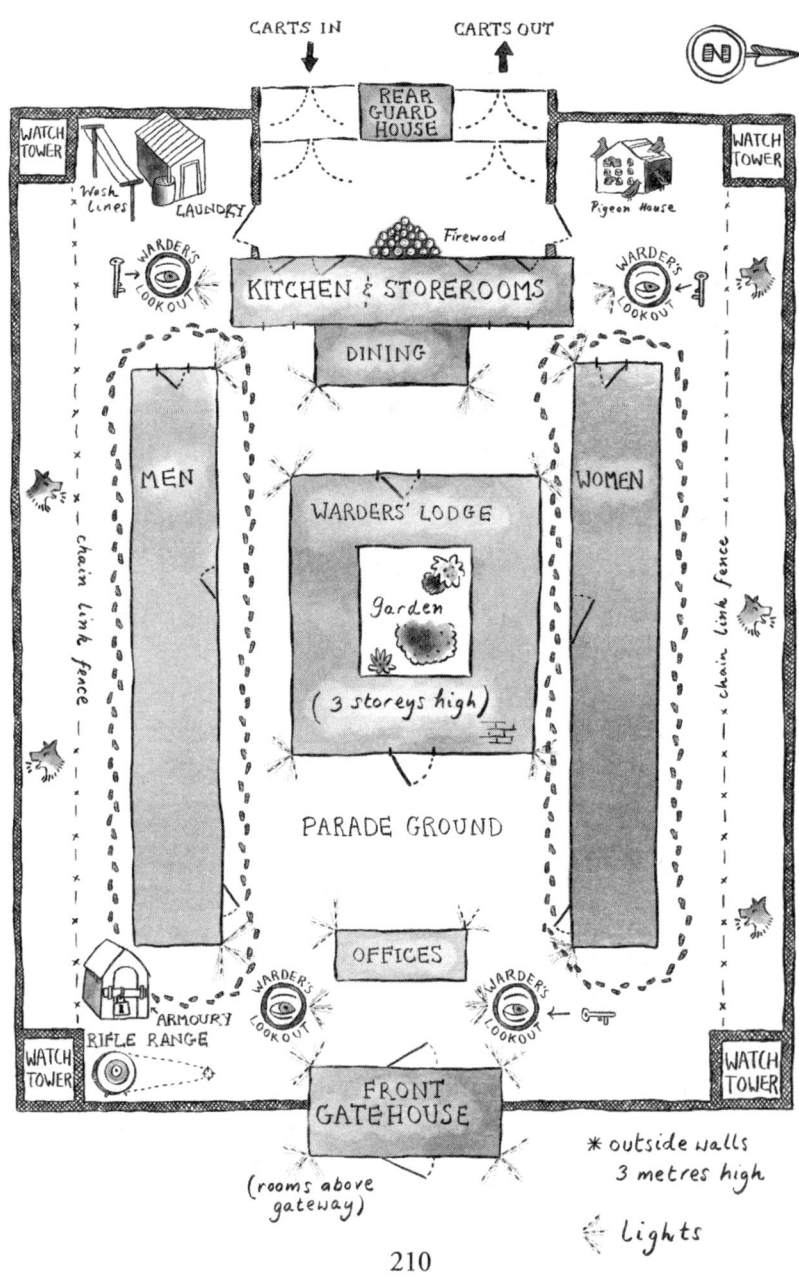

Lysander came by with a large piece of paper on which he'd listed the order of events for his show, with the timings. The show was to start at 8 o'clock.

"Can you set off a few fireworks earlier to remind the prison warders about the show tonight?" asked Vivi.

"Easy," said Lysander.

"We've made millions of armbands." Humphrey tossed an armful of red strips into the air and they rained onto him. "I've got stripes. I'm a red tiger."

"Hey—pick them up before the chickens poo on them," said Joe.

Humphrey helped Lysander stuff them into a shoulder bag. "I'll pass them along the whisper-chain in my quarter. Everyone wants one."

"Voh'mah berrin," they called. "Luck be with you."

He hadn't been gone long when Nomie arrived to drop off some things Vivi needed, and Stracky drove his cart into the field at the front of the house. Joe went to investigate. Several people were loading the cart with haybales from the haystack.

"Do you need any help?" he called.

He was surprised when they said yes. Next thing he was on the back of the cart, helping Stracky slide the heavy bales into the hands of one of Stracky's older brothers, who piled them up. It was hard, hot work.

"What do you need them for?" asked Joe, panting.

"For getting into the prison," said Stracky.

Then it grew dark. The preparations for the prison were over. It was nearly time to go.

Chapter Twenty-Nine

Lysander's Performance

No one could sit still. Vivi rubbed Doris's levers with a greasy rag. Joe followed Hessa's instructions and filled a bag with snacks and three lanterns with oil. They all put on warm jackets and Sal hung the lumpy bag that Nomie had brought on the handles of Vivi's chair.

Joe swung Humphrey around. "Fireworks! Are you excited Humpty-Dumpty? I'm so excited."

Vivi made sure they each had a strip of red cloth and spares in their pocket. "When you see other people wearing them, tie one around your upper arm."

Sal was going with Vivi in case she needed a push, since Hessa couldn't.

"I'm sad not to see the rescue, but I'll see the fireworks after all," said Hessa.

Vivi rolled into Magnus's shed and emerged with the hawk standing, hooded, on the back of her chair. "Because of the pigeons," she explained.

Hessa took Vivi's hand in her good one. She touched first her own, and then Vivi's forehead with their clasped hands. "Voh'mah berrin. Luck be with you. And please don't get arrested."

Sal took a lantern and she and Vivi set off.

"Where are they going?" asked Humphrey.

"They've got something to do," said Joe. "We'll meet them later."

Joe and Francie carried the other lanterns and Hessa held Humphrey's hand. They joined the stream of lights bobbing along the dark road towards town. They headed for the paint workshop as Hessa said that was where the family always watched the fireworks from. It had a great view of Mina Mendalwar, and it was a little back from the crowd along the river bank, which was better for Francie. They arranged themselves in a row with their backs against the workshop wall and started on the snacks.

"Always before, we've watched the show together." Hessa sounded wistful. "Mama and Papa, Vivi and me, and the aunts."

Humphrey wrapped his arms round her legs.

She patted his back. "Thanks, Humph."

They watched two Custodians walk along the river path.

"They know we have fireworks on Hallowmas Eve, but they don't know that everything is different this year. So exciting!"

They'd finished the cheese puffs and started on the pugnut cookies when Hessa shouted and pointed. Auntie Pi was coming—with Ma in a wheelchair! They had a big hug. Humphrey snuggled onto Ma's lap. Francie sat on the ground and leaned against Ma's legs and rubbed her cheek on Ma's knee.

The reflections of the lanterns in the miners' camp flickered on the river; they could see the men sitting round their fires talking and singing. The men had no idea that children were waiting, hidden under the trees of Mina Mendalwar.

They told Ma that Sal was helping Vivi, but she didn't get to ask any questions as the first streak of light flew up from the top of Mina Mendalwar. It seemed to hang there before vanishing, and was followed by several loud bangs and white lights dropped from high up. The spectators cheered and clapped at this signal that soon the performance would start. The men down in the camp stood up and moved around, trying to see what was going on.

They had just passed a bag of dried peaches along the row when they heard a soft metallic rumble. It grew and grew. Francie put her hands over her ears, even though she already had cotton wool in them. The noise said "something scary is about to happen". The hairs on Joe's arms crept up, even though he knew it was Madoc rolling something round inside an empty drum. The rumble died away and was replaced by a deep drum beat, *buh-boom, buh-boom*. Madoc again. It sounded like the beating heart of the hill. White shapes appeared at the summit and began to drift down through the trees, illuminated from below by small flares on the ground.

When the workmen caught sight of the white shapes floating towards them, they shouted and pointed.

"That's not really ghosts," Joe told Humph and Ma. "It's Idris, Etta, Lilja, Max and the others. They're walking down the path, holding up brooms with sheets over them."

Buh-boom, buh-boom. The drum beat went steadily on. Lights streaked in a curve over the miners' camp and disappeared, accompanied by scalp-tingling screeches. Some of the river-bank crowd yelped. Their voices were echoed by more screeches from under the trees, and fireworks exploding all over the hill.

A white fog began to billow above the trees and a huge face appeared in it, mouth open in a fierce snarl. Everyone gasped. Joe would have been petrified if he hadn't recognised Lysander's face, and remembered that Etta was projecting it onto the fog using mirrors. Humphrey buried his face in Joe's tummy, then turned his head so he could see out of half an eye the next stream of ghostly figures floating down the hill and vanishing.

The crowd held its breath as voices, some soft, some loud, swirled around the gravestones, more and more joining in, a mass muttering that rolled off the hill.

"What're they saying?" whispered Humphrey.

"They're saying 'Leave now' and 'Go home'," said Hessa.

As the fog swelled and rose above the hill, like smoke from a volcano, it was accompanied by a jangle of bells, gongs and cymbals. Humphrey held his ears.

"Madoc's very good at making scary music, isn't he?" said Joe.

The sound effects became louder and faster, and the fog grew and grew, until it seemed to tip over and roll slowly down the hill. It halted over the camp, muffling the workmen's reactions. When it thinned, the camp was in complete darkness and silence. The fog had smothered the fires, putting out every single lantern and candle.

Joe shivered. He imagined the men clustering together,

frightened. He felt sorry for them. It wasn't their idea to make a hole through Mina Mendalwar.

More fireworks burst golden around the campsite.

"Look!" Hessa pointed just down the river path. A Custodian on horseback seemed to be telling two other Custodians to go to the Mina and investigate. Although he gestured and waved his sword, they turned and ran towards the town.

Joe noticed something else. Francie had escaped the noise of the fireworks. She had slid down until she was lying with her eyes open, staring at the sky. She was flying.

Up and up, into the middle of the dancing, spinning fragments of light. Into the silence. Stars burst into more stars just beyond reach. A green streak shoots past and hangs, hangs, hangs before shrinking into not-quite nothing.

Down below, the trees of Mina Mendalwar are swaying. There's no wind, but they are bowing and waving to something. Soft shapes are pouring from between the trees' roots. They swell and they shrink; they shift, nudge and merge. Several become one and then separate and elongate.

The shifting shapes pour down the hill between the trees, more and more of them. They hug the ground and have no light; the men in the camp can't see them coming. When they reach the men they flow over and around them, nuzzling them, enfolding them. They flood the men's memories, reminding them of what they've lost and what they've left behind.

The men look around, at each other. Everything's changed. They go into their tents, come out with their packs. They pick up their tools and walk away from the camp, smiling and laughing because they're going home.

The shapes flow beside the men as far as the road, then turn back to Mina Mendalwar. They slip up the slope under the trees, slide between the roots and dissolve back into the earth.

Above, the sky is filled with flowers that bud, bloom, burst and colour the sky. Pink becomes red. Yellow becomes orange. Everything turns golden.

Chapter Thirty

Meanwhile...

Doris was tucked into the shadows just off the road with Magnus standing, unmoving, on one of the levers. Sal watched the road and bounced on her toes. A hundred metres away, she could just make out the shape of the prison.

"Where is he?" she said for the third or fourth time. "The whole plan's going to be ruined before it's even started." To make matters worse, she could suddenly see for miles as the moon emerged from between clouds. "I thought it was going to be a dark night!" She tried not to screech. "You said, 'Thank goodness there are clouds.'"

"More clouds would be better. On the other hand, it'll be quite good *not* having to wait for a firework to see where you are," said Vivi. "Let's put our armbands on."

They each tied a strip of red cloth on the other's arm and pulled their black cloaks around themselves. They weren't really cloaks—just large pieces of black fabric with head-holes that Ronia had donated for night-time camouflage.

The first flash of the Hallowmas fireworks shot into the sky and hung there.

"And now," said Vivi, "everything begins."

After the flash, the bangs that followed sounded like gunfire. Warders waving lanterns ran out of the front gatehouse to see what was happening. They must have remembered it was Hallowmas when they saw white lights drifting down the sky. One or two turned back, but others seemed to agree that they could leave their posts for a while to see the show. They hurried out of the gate and along the road towards Cruxcia.

"Eleven of them," said Sal. "That's eleven fewer warders inside the prison."

Vivi took off Magnus's hood and whispered to him, "If they set off messenger pigeons, Magnus, you must kill them. We don't want those warders sending to the Custodians for reinforcements."

She unclipped his leash and Magnus spread his vast wings. The air shivered as he soared into the night. Sal shivered, too. She was glad she wouldn't be able to see him snatching the poor pigeons out of the sky.

"Shhh. Someone's coming," Vivi whispered.

Three people were approaching, and, as they passed, Sal could see that the two on the outside were Custodians. The large man walking between them had his hands behind his back. Handcuffed? As they got close to the prison he started singing loudly. Sal hardly breathed until they'd disappeared through the prison gate.

"That explains why he's late," said Vivi.

"Was that him? Stracky's father?"

"It was. And that song's called 'Don't Give Up'." Vivi snapped the lid of her father's pocket watch shut. "You'll have to throw the meat. There's no time to find someone else to do it."

Sal panicked. "But I can't—I'm a useless thrower."

"Of course you can. You just have to get the bones over the wall. You know where to go. Then, when the dogs are quiet, find the others and let them know."

"I can't—"

"Go!"

There was no arguing with Vivi. Sal unhooked the bag of bloody beef bones from Doris's handles. She'd try—for Pa.

"They may need you to go over the wall too, now they haven't got Stracky's father."

They might! Sal's stomach churned with excitement and terror. "You'll be left here on your own."

"Not for long. I'll be fine," said Vivi. "Luck be with you."

Sal set off for the prison wall. Lights shone out of the gatehouse, but all the windows in the watchtowers were dark and blank. She waited until thick cloud covered the moon again, pulled the black fabric up to cover her head, then forced herself to leave the road and run across the open space towards the prison wall. She tried to imagine she was invisible. No voice yelled at her to stop, no gun went off. She only heard men laughing in the distance and an occasional bark. She could just make out the two nearest watchtowers against the sky, marking the corners of the prison walls.

A sharp bark from the other side of the wall made her jump.

This was terrifying. Quick. Get it over with. She opened the bag with shaking fingers.

Nomie had laced five meaty bones, each with enough tranquiliser to make a dog very dozy. Sal picked up the first bone and hurled it. It bounced off the wall just above her head, leaving a bloody mark. This was ridiculous. She hadn't magically acquired throwing skills. None at all. She had warned Vivi.

She threw again, and again, and again, and each time the bone landed somewhere near her feet—mostly behind her. She had to feel around for it, and it grew gritty with dirt. If she ever got it over the wall the dogs would probably refuse to touch it. She was useless at throwing. Why was she the one doing this?

The dogs were growling and barking. They could hear her—could probably smell the bones. Someone would come and investigate if she didn't hurry. Missed again. She wanted to cry. She was ready to dump the bones and run.

Then she heard Ma's voice in her head: *Stop. When it doesn't work the first few times, take three deep breaths and ask yourself, "Can I try it another way?"* That was Ma when Sal was having trouble with a mathematical problem. She squatted down and took some breaths. How could she do this differently? She could try standing side-on, like a discus thrower, with the bone in her right hand and the wall to her left. She pictured the parabola she wanted the bone to follow, curving high over the wall.

She stood and took the bone by its knobbly end. She swung her arm back, then flung it up. The bone sailed over! How did that happen? The next one didn't, nor the one after, but then two in a row went over. The dogs snapped and snarled—they must be fighting over the meat. It took three more attempts to get the fourth bone over, then Sal heard another noise.

Voices. Coming towards her. Whoever they were, they had a lantern and weren't trying to hide, so prison warders, or Custodians. Maybe they'd heard the dogs. They couldn't have seen her yet; she was well beyond their circle of light. She tiptoed away from the wall and out onto the dark plain.

When she was far enough away from the light she ducked down under the black cloth, hoping that if the moon shone she'd look like a bush or a boulder. She was still gripping the last bone. She didn't dare drop it in case a bird pecked at it and died. The lantern-light bobbed along below the wall until it was under the far watchtower, then the light swept over the ground. They must be looking for something —not a person then, something small. Maybe something had dropped from the tower window. She wished they'd hurry up and find it because Stracky and his crew would be here any minute.

At last, laughter. The lantern swung around, then the voices were on their way back. One of them said: "…would have meant trouble."

After that, the only faint light on the plain came from behind the prison wall. Sal crept towards it, groping with her hands until she felt its hard surface. She listened for the dogs. Silence. Then a snort, and a doggy snore. It had worked!

Now where was Stracky? It was so dark. She listened for clues but could hear nothing. Were they here?

As she felt her way towards the corner she sensed a soft thud ahead. Then another, and another. Then a tiny metallic jingle.

She tiptoed forward, and there was Stracky, standing at his horse's head.

"The dogs are asleep," she whispered.

He nodded and went to tell the people unloading the cart. The cloud thinned a little and in the starlight she saw people with armbands hauling bales of hay off the cart and heaving them against the wall. They worked fast, without speaking, building a staircase, three bales by four for the base, eight for the next layer. The bales kept coming.

Stracky came back to his horse and Sal gave him the bad news. "I'm afraid your father's not coming. He's been arrested. We saw him being marched in the main gate."

His shoulders sagged and he turned away for a moment and sniffed.

"Sorry," she added, feeling very feeble.

He turned back to her. "Even more reason to get every prisoner out." He beckoned over a young woman called Ali. She and Stracky's father were supposed to be working together tonight. Did Sal know where the laundry building was? Good. Because Sal could show Ali.

"We're going first," whispered Ali. "You lead the way. Ready?"

Sal thought she might throw up, she was so scared. But there was no time to think. The hay steps on this side were finished. More of the heavy bales were being swung over the wall. Once a few had been dropped over, two people followed with cutting tools. Ali climbed onto the wall, and Sal followed up the wide staircase, jumped down the other side and landed on the bales.

She was inside the prison! They were in the fenced dog run

next to the wall. How long would the dogs sleep? She tossed the last bone in their direction and wiped her hand on her cloak. As soon as the cutters had made a big enough hole, Sal and Ali squirmed through the wire.

They crossed the open space ahead, over the scuffed surface of the exercise track to the long back wall of the male prisoners' dormitories. They turned left along the wall, close under the eaves to the corner, where they stopped. Waited. Checked around. Listened.

Sal tried to orient herself. She'd looked at the plan of the prison enough times, but suddenly she couldn't visualise it. Everything was unfamiliar in real life, on the ground, in the dark. She recognised the nearest shape as the lookout. The lamp on top of it cast a cone of light that didn't quite reach the fence. The wall on the right was the cookhouse—unless it was the dining room. Think. The laundry should be beyond the lookout, but she couldn't see it.

As they waited, the sky exploded red and yellow. They pressed themselves to the wall. The fireworks faded.

Clattering pots—definitely the cookhouse.

Ali put her face close to Sal's. Ready to run? she asked with her eyebrows. Sal nodded, then they were running, behind the cone of light, to the back of the lookout. They paused. The warder was only centimetres away through the wall.

A door opened and closed somewhere. Footsteps. Sal held her breath. The warder in the lookout called something, someone answered and they both laughed, then the footsteps were moving away.

The laundry building was a few steps further. Sal felt her way to the door. Ali had a pick-lock tool ready, but when Sal tried the handle it wasn't locked. They pulled it shut behind them. Sal put out her hands, shuffled blindly forward and banged up against something large and metallic that clanged.

Ali hissed at her.

Another firework lit the sky briefly and showed taps and tubs and some sort of machinery. Through an open door, another room was lined with shelves of folded cloth.

Uniforms. But were they yellow or brown? Ali held one to the small window. A shirt, impossible to tell what colour, but definitely a warder's because it had lots of pockets. She lit a match and held it close to the shelves. The top two held brown clothes. They pulled some down. Heavy cotton trousers on the top shelf, shirts on the one below. They filled two laundry baskets with a pile of each, then they abandoned their black cloaks and pulled warders' pants and shirts over their clothes.

Creamy moonlight crossed the room for a moment. Ali had transformed into a warder; they both snorted back horrified laughs. Now to transform everyone else.

They tried to walk casually to the gap in the fence, as if they were supposed to be there, though Sal's heart was hammering so fast she thought she was having a heart attack. Breathe, Sal, breathe. The hole in the fence was much bigger now, no need to bend to get through, and the steps on this side were finished. Up the hay bales, over and down. A dozen people waiting. They pounced on the clothes and moments later were dressed as warders.

Sal and Ali knelt on the top step and watched as the "warders" went through the fence with their tools and then split up. Some went to open the male dormitories, some to the women's building, and some were going to the armoury. Sal thought of Hessa on the ground with blood pouring down her arm. No shooting. Please, no more shooting.

"What now?" Sal whispered.

"Now we wait," said Ali. "Then we help people over the wall, point them towards Cruxcia and tell them to run."

"Have you got family in there?" asked Sal.

"My mother, brother and auntie."

A boom, a streak and an explosion of silver and gold stars floated down. It was glorious. Breathtaking.

Then they waited. And waited.

Strange noises echoed around the valley from Lysander's show.

Here, nothing. Time had stopped. Nothing. Nothing. Sal counted seconds in her head. Four minutes. Five minutes.

At last, a shadow materialised through the hole in the fence, then another—prisoners! Eight men ran to the steps and scrambled over. Ali knew one and hugged him; none of them was Pa, or Ali's brother.

At the same time, a voice shouted in the distance.

The sky clouded over again. Two pricks of lantern light were moving across the prison yard towards the main gate. Sal held her breath—please don't let them be discovered. Ali gave the freed men red armbands. They wanted to wait for more prisoners, but she pointed towards Cruxcia and told them to get going. People weren't risking their lives so they could all be recaptured.

When they'd vanished into the night, Ali joined Sal at the top of the steps. They peered into the darkness. Lanterns were moving across the grounds, fast. People running. Warders! Two blasts on a whistle. Whatever was happening, it wasn't in the plan.

A man darted through the fence and over the hay bales. He was wearing a brown uniform, but he took off the shirt to reveal his red armband. He spoke fast. "Some women have been caught. They've ordered a headcount of all prisoners."

Ali was hovering on the top step. She made a decision. "We need to distract them. I'm going back over. I'll start a fire."

The man argued with her, but didn't offer a better idea.

"I'll come with you," said Sal. Anything would be better than waiting here. They were over the wall again and through the fence. Then Ali pointed Sal towards the laundry, and indicated that she was going the other way. She was gone.

Sal had meant they'd make a fire together. Instead, she was alone in the prison. Her legs felt watery. She didn't have matches. Maybe Cruxcians always carried a box in their pocket. Sal ran to the end of the male dormitory. Voices came from inside. She took a deep breath and walked purposefully across the open space to the cookhouse.

Someone was coming up behind her. She glanced round. A warder. She held steady.

"Hey, you!" he hailed her. "Take an urgent message to Latimer. Tell him to bring his tools straight to the armoury. Someone's glued the locks."

Sal nodded and said, "Straight away, sir," to be on the safe side, but he had gone. Astonishing. She'd just passed herself off as a warder. And glue in the locks! No guns. How clever was that?

Where to find matches? She peered in the cookhouse door. There was another door inside. Why not be brave? She pushed it open and was startled to see a woman in an apron, sitting in the gloom at a table having a drink.

She glanced up at Sal. "What d'you want?"

Sal gulped. "Got any matches?"

"On the shelf by the stove. Mind you bring them back." The woman poured something from a bottle into her mug. "What's going on out there? Someone lost the plot?"

"Looks like it," Sal slipped a box into her pocket. "Thanks."

"Do us a favour," the woman called. "Put that lot in the lamp room for me, would you?" She jerked her head towards the end of the room.

That lot was a crate full of sparkling glass—the chimneys from a dozen oil lamps, all newly washed. Sal carried it carefully through the door at the end of the kitchen and found herself in a storeroom. A storeroom for everything needed to light the prison: shelves of lamps and candles, boxes of wicks, and bottles and drums full of lamp oil, all illuminated by a lamp hanging from the ceiling. Would lamp oil be good for starting a fire? She wasn't sure, but at the end of the shelf were red labels that said DANGER FIRE HAZARD. Perfect. She took two of the dangerous bottles.

At the back of the lamp room there was another door. Sal slid the bolt back and stepped out into the service yard where the delivery carts were unloaded. The firewood Francie had seen being delivered was stacked against the wall, and beyond it was a bin full of kindling. Sal threw together a pile of kindling in the corner between the kitchen wall and the wood stack, with large bits of bark and small logs around it, and lots of room for air, as Pa had taught her. Then she poured one of the bottles of hazardous liquid over the kindling, and the other up the side of the woodpile. She held a match to the kindling. Nothing, nothing, then—

Whoosh! She jumped back as the fire burst into life more fiercely than she'd imagined possible. She smelled singed hair. Flames licked over to the woodpile. In no time the paint on the outside wall of the kitchen was melting and emitting foul fumes.

In less than a minute the flames were taller than Sal. She had to get away, quickly. She couldn't go back through the cookhouse—she could hear shouting and boots running in there—nor through the locked double gates at the back. She was trapped.

"Hey!" A voice yelled from the rear gatehouse. A door banged. Figures came towards her through the smoke. "Stop."

She swerved and ran, yelling, "Fire!" Two brown uniforms burst through a small side gate. They were dragging a hose. She ducked past them and followed the hose through the gate. She was facing another warder's lookout and, beyond, the women's dormitory.

Women were filing out of the building and being directed by two women warders with truncheons to sit in rows on the grass. The prisoners were coughing, and shouted at the warders that they needed to get further away from the smoke, which was coming from Ali's fire as well as Sal's.

Suddenly all the warders seemed to realise that there was more than one fire. Any order vanished into chaos. Bells rang, whistles blew, and warders screamed orders at each other as they ran in panic between the buildings.

One of the two women warders disappeared into the billows of smoke. Sal saw her chance. She ran up to the remaining warder. "Latimer says you're needed at the armoury, quick as you can." And the warder just nodded, and went!

Thirty scared faces looked at Sal—including a familiar one. "Tash! Shala. All of you. Pretend I'm actually a warder and follow me. Hang onto each other, come on."

But which way, when every way looked dangerous? The far end of the women's dormitory was on fire, and smoke was billowing all around them. Burning timbers spat sparks onto the dry grass near the wall, setting it on fire. The unsedated dogs on this side barked and howled.

Sal pulled the neck of her top over her nose and grabbed Tash's hand. They bent low and ran through the smoke between the two fires. They were all coughing and Sal's eyes were streaming as they ran past the dining room and the corner of the cookhouse, to the door at the top of the men's dormitory. It was standing wide.

She yelled, "Anyone still in there? This way, hurry!" but her voice echoed through an empty building.

The women could now see other prisoners running through smoke to the hole in the fence. They followed them to the hay bales. No one tried to stop them.

The bales were falling apart because so many people had

swarmed over already, but the women helped each other to scramble up the slippery hay and hurl themselves over the wall.

Sal followed. People were waiting on the other side—dozens of people, with more arriving all the time, hugging and cheering, all with red armbands. Sal pulled off her brown shirt so her armband showed, and scanned the faces. Pa? Pa? Was he here? Had he got out?

"Everything all right?" It was Ronia.

"I'm fine—but I can't find Pa! And someone needs to get the dogs out, they're trapped."

Ronia nodded. "It's okay. We got the sedated ones out. Nomie and others have gone with tranquilisers to get the rest. They'll wake up in our barn tomorrow and not know how they got there."

Half of Cruxcia seemed to be milling around on the plain beyond the prison, every one of them wearing a red armband. Together they made a shield for the escapers against the guards and Custodians.

Sal stood on the remains of the hay to look for Pa. Light from the fires flickered over people but she couldn't pick out individual faces. No Pa. There'd be no prison left by the time those fires were put out. Were all the prisoners safe? Please let them be safe. And the warders. They'd only meant to distract them, not murder them.

A few warders raced towards them waving lanterns and truncheons, but they slowed to a walk when they realised how big the crowd was. Then they stopped. Discussed what they should do. And backed away.

The crowd moved towards the road. Sal skirted round the outside, checking faces as she went. Somewhere ahead of her a single voice started singing: "*Free-ee all Cruxcians. Free-ee-dom for Cruxcia.*" It was Vivi. And hundreds of voices joined in, singing in harmony: "*Free-ee all Cruxcians. Free-ee-dom for Cruxcia.*"

Sal's skin tingled all over, and a great lump swelled in her throat. Then the world was filled with colour. Giant flowers swelled and grew across the sky in pink, yellow, red and gold, followed by the boom of their detonation. Sal stood and stared up at the grand finale of Lysander's show.

She was crying—and then a hand took her shoulder.

She was beyond the edge of the crowd and for a moment she thought a warder had got her. She tensed, about to wriggle and run, but a familiar voice said: "Sal? Is it my Sal?"

"Pa!" She fell into her father's arms.

Everyone followed the singing—the prisoners who'd climbed the hay bales, the people who'd helped them escape, and those who'd come to meet them. They walked together, singing. They met the warders coming back from the fireworks; they knew they had no power against so many. Besides, the warders could smell the smoke and see the flames. They were worried about their workmates, and whether there'd be a bed for them tonight.

The warders were given the same message all along the line: "Take a red arm armband and join us, or get to the Sky Worff while you can." A few tied armbands on and joined the singers flowing into town.

Pa and Sal caught up with Vivi, who was smiling and holding Tash's hand while being pushed by a beaming man, her father

Taliesin. We're like a family river, Sal thought, growing as we travel. First only Sal, then Sal and Pa, now Sal, Pa, Vivi, Tash and Taliesin.

All around them, people peered hopefully in the dim light, and called out names, found each other, hugged and cried. The whisper-chain worked its way through the crowd. Every servant at Mundle's Mansion had gone on strike, and his waterpipes had been turned off. The first dirigible would take off at dawn with the miners. Ronia was taking twenty helpers up to the mansion to make sure Mundle, Abercrombie and Zander actually left.

And then their river grew bigger as familiar shapes came barrelling out of the darkness. Humphrey, Joe and Francie threw themselves at Pa. Then Ma was out of her wheelchair and crying, Pa was hugging Ma and crying, Hessa clung tight to Taliesin, who was trying to mind her shoulder—and also crying. Auntie Pi steered the empty wheelchair and handed out handkerchiefs.

They walked along the road with their arms round each other. There was so much to tell.

"The GTC bribed the judge. Vivi's submission to the Land Court was brilliant," said Hessa.

"I wish I'd heard it," said Tash.

"Sal worked out that the GTC's planning to flood our valley," said Vivi.

"Joe got your map tube from Odo, Pa, and Francie finished the map of the valley," said Sal.

"And then Francie saw the place in the mountains they were going to send you," said Joe. Francie squeezed his arm. "She's very glad you're not going there. So am I."

"I used sharp scissors. I made a million of these." Humphrey waved his armband.

"He did. Millions and millions," said Hessa.

"Francie made a plan of the prison," said Vivi. "That's what made the whole rescue possible."

Francie looked at the sky and smiled.

"Vivi overheard that the GTC were moving the prisoners on Hallowmas Day, so we knew we had to get you out," said Sal.

"Stracky thought of the hay-bale stairs," said Hessa.

"Glue in the locks was Hessa's idea," said Vivi. "Genius."

"You were all part of it, you all made it happen," said Taliesin. "I can't tell you how wonderful it feels to walk along the road with you like this."

"Hear, hear," Pa threw his arms wide. "We're free! And all thanks to our astonishing children."

"Here we are," said Sal as they went through the gate into the yard of the kaleidoscope house, "all of us. All together."

"How many all?" demanded Carrot, flying out of the tree and landing on the table.

"Eleven, so far," said Joe. "There's more we haven't met yet."

From the top of the wall Magnus called a greeting. He was home, too.

That night Pa borrowed a sleeping bag and the Santanders snuggled up in a row on the roof under the stars. It was hard to sleep because they all kept thinking of one more thing they had to ask—or tell.

"Is that why you came to Cruxcia, Pa, because you wanted to find family?"

"It was my secret hope. When Taliesin and Kestor joined me in the prison we worked it out."

Ma was lying with her head on Pa's chest. "You're bonier than you were. We'll have to feed you up."

"With kleffi," said Humphrey sleepily.

"Are you really better, Angelica?" Pa asked.

"One hundred percent," said Ma. "Everything's all right now."

"Having Pa back is the best thing ever," said Joe.

Chapter Thirty-One

The Sky Worff

In the morning, the whisper-chain passed on message after message; poor Stracky was out of breath delivering them. Hessa and Vivi took it in turns to go to the neighbours and pass the messages on. The first important one was that all of the prisoners had got out of the prison safely. A few warders had suffered burns, but none had been badly hurt.

The second message said that most of the Custodians had gone. Zander and Abercrombie had ordered them to arrest Mundle, but they refused to arrest anyone because they hadn't been properly paid for ages. So Zander sacked them, and they said they were leaving anyway. The miners had gone in the first dirigible and the Custodians and warders were queuing for the next one.

"That explains why there weren't many Custodians around last night," said Sal.

The next message reported that Mundle's hangers-on, the mumazus, had fled from Mundle's mansion. Their ornithopter could hardly get airborne, it was so overloaded with jewellery and loot.

Then they heard that all the food from the mansion's pantry was being taken to the Societies' Meeting Hall for a Hallowmas feast and party tonight.

Besides the whisper-chain messages, one came by pigeon: *Bring your rope tonight, Joe. From Lysander*

Everyone in the kaleidoscope house wanted to be sure that Mundle left, so those with enough energy walked down to the Sky Worff to see him off. Joe and Francie walked with Pa, who kept looking at them and smiling. "Look at you," he kept saying quietly, "just look at you both!"

"We're up to your chin," said Joe.

"You are," said Pa. He put his arms around their shoulders. "You know, my heart soared when I saw your message painted on the hill. I'd begun to despair. I thought I'd never see you again. I was afraid you'd think I'd deserted you."

Joe shook his head. "No. We never thought that. None of us. Not for a single moment."

It was true. Francie nodded vigorous agreement.

They kicked a stone down the road between them, just like the old days, until it got lost in a ditch.

"Tell me," said Pa, "how did you manage? I left so little money for you all. I had nightmares of you being cold and hungry."

Joe laughed. "We were cold and hungry a few times on the Great Race. But it was worth it. We won—it gave us enough gold to come and find you."

"My word," said Pa. "Angelica took you on the Great Race?"

"No. Ma wasn't there, we lost her on the way to the start. The four of us went on without her."

"You children did the Great Race without your mother—and survived, and won?" Pa stood stock still and stared at Joe and Francie. "The four of you?"

"Us and another boy called Beckett. Francie made the best maps anyone had ever seen. We won all the prize money, because some of the grown-up teams cheated. The Cowboys, and Monty and his Mountaineers, Keith Skinner and the rest. And it's the same here—Mundle and Tall and Short, they lied and cheated too."

"Some people only want to win and they don't care how," said Pa.

"They think winning's just about them," said Joe. "But it's not, it's about everybody."

"That's exactly right." Pa squeezed their arms. "You know I dreamed about walking along with you like this. Thank you for rescuing me."

"We've still got loads of gold left, and me and Francie really want to use some of it to buy a mountain and keep it for bears and wolves and eagles to live on."

"An excellent plan," said Pa.

They followed Hessa and her parents onto the landing strip, where people were waiting with spades and wrenches to put the Sky Worff out of action. The last few Custodians were queuing to board, including Private Clocksley.

"Just think," said Pa, "if Mundle and the GTC had had their way, I'd be getting into that dirigible now, to be taken to a cold, wet prison camp in the mountains."

"Instead of which, we can wave goodbye to Custodians and prison warders," said Joe. "We've got rid of them all!"

He went over to talk to Clocksley, who said he was going home and glad of it. "Why was Loofus so determined to arrest us?" asked Joe.

"Loofus wanted the reward," Clocksley explained. "When those GTC bosses, Zander and Abercrombie, found out that Judge Scumble was doing the Land Court hearing, they panicked. They knew how much gold it would take to bribe him. They thought if no other mapmakers came to Cruxcia, the court case would go ahead uncontested and they'd save a barrel of coins."

"Mundle would win without having to bribe the judge?"

"Ex-act-ly. They offered a hundred gold pieces to any Custodian who apprehended a mapmaker. But since Loofus and I kept it secret that your mother was a mapmaker, we were the only ones after you."

"I'm sorry you're going home empty-handed," said Joe.

"Not me," said Clocksley. "I've got two bags full of kleffi!" He waved from the top of the steps and climbed on board.

The Santanders and the Terrabynds found themselves a spot near the launch pad. A huge cheer went up as the last dirigible was unmoored from the tower and rose slowly into the sky. The last remaining ornithopter trundled out onto the landing strip and waited, wings outstretched.

A movement rippled through the crowd as a carriage drove up. Abercrombie and Zander climbed out and stamped round, swearing and poking people with accusing fingers when they discovered that Mundle's mumazus had stolen their ornithopter. The crowd just laughed, which made them even angrier.

"Don't worry, we'll be back," Clarice Abercrombie yelled. "The GTC will return, and next time we'll be armed with cannons and revolvers."

"We'll keep a lookout for you, then," shouted a voice from the crowd.

"We'll build a prison that none of you will escape from," said Norton Zander. "You'll be sorry."

"Dream on!" Hessa shouted, and everyone laughed.

"Bye," they called. "We won't miss you."

Tall and Short climbed on board the last ornithopter, which continued to sit on the landing strip.

At last the governor's maroon and cream carriage drove up. All the luggage was unloaded, but Mundle held up a hand: he wanted to say something before he boarded.

Everyone hushed each other, and pushed closer to hear.

"I understand why you are sending me into exile. You are jealous of me! You envy my brains, my power, my popularity and my beautiful things. Without me, and the GTC, Cruxcia is nothing. I have done more for you than any Cruxcian before me, but I don't expect praise. I will go to Porto Pearls, but I'm not going away. The GTC isn't going away either. Other parts of Grania have accepted the GTC and some helpful people have become extremely rich. You'll soon be begging the GTC to return. Meanwhile, you ungrateful peasants, I hope you all rot."

Someone in the crowd started singing the "Moustache Man" song and everyone joined in.

Finally, finally, Malvicious Mundle climbed from the carriage and into the ornithopter. Those close enough heard Clarice Abercrombie yelling at him and Mundle blustering back, then the door was shut. The rubber launch rope was wound back and the ornithopter was propelled into the air.

As the wings began to flap and the ornithopter rose above the crowd, seven horses galloped onto the Sky Worff. Seven Cowboys looked around and realised that the last dirigible and the last ornithopter had left without them.

"Where's Mundle? We haven't been paid!" shouted Cody Cole.

"Noooo. It's not fair," shouted another. "Some meddlers scattered our horses—they deserve to be skinned."

"How will we get to Porto Pearls? Our horses can't cross the desert," bellowed a third.

"I know it's not kind to be glad when others are upset," said Joe. "But if those Cowboys get their comeuppance, this whole town will be so happy. I'll tell you all about them on the way home. Oh Pa, we've got so many stories for you, but we'd better wait for Sal and Humphrey. They'll want to tell, too."

As they went through the market on the way back, Francie pointed to an enclosure and hid her face in Pa's chest. The Cowboys were taking the saddles off their horses. They were trying to exchange horses for camels, but they wanted money as well. The camel woman shook her head and started to lead the camels away, and after some swearing, the Cowboys handed over the reins.

Joe and Hessa climbed on a railing for a better view and

Francie got brave enough to climb up too, with Pa standing beside her. They all enjoyed watching the Cowboys scrambling up onto the camels, only to fall straight off the other side. The angrier the Cowboys got, the quicker the camels tipped them off.

Tash laughed. "The camels are training them to be gentle and patient. I think it's going to take them a while."

Chapter Thirty-Two

The Party

There had never been a party like the one that began late that afternoon. A stream of carts delivered sides of meat, wheels of cheese, sacks of vegetables, whole hams and boxes of chocolates from the pantry in Mundle's mansion to the Societies' Hall. Every cook spent the day peeling and chopping, roasting and baking. Chairs and tables were carried out into the square. Stracky's cart was parked at one end for a stage, and musicians fetched their instruments. Lanterns and bunting were strung up, and the banners from the hall were unhooked and rehung between the trees. All around the square, family groups hugged and talked and laughed.

Nomie, Auntie Pi and Tash pushed three tables together. Ma held Pa's hand and they sat talking quietly and taking everything in. They both looked thinner and more wrinkled, but they couldn't stop smiling. There were lots of people for them to meet: Lysander and his parents Kerala and Kestor (who Pa knew from prison), and Lysander's two older sisters, and their small children—who persuaded Humphrey off Pa's lap and into a game of tag around the trees.

Pa sat beside Aunt Clarrie, grandma of Hessa, Vivi and Lysander; it was she who had rescued Sal from Clocksley and Loofus. She beckoned Joe over and he stood close to Pa. "Joe, it's so good to finally meet you. You look like your grandfather. It's as if he were here, aged twelve. Oh my." She dabbed her eyes with her hankie. "Tell me, Joe, what sort of boy are you? What do you like doing most?"

Joe considered. "I like exploring. I'm going to be a routefinder like Pa. But I'll only go exploring if Francie wants to come. Francie needs her family."

Francie had leaned against Pa for a while, rubbing her cheek against the top of his head, but now she was sitting apart from the group, drawing them all. Hessa and Vivi's dad Taliesin stood behind her and watched for a minute, then he looked over at Pa, nodding and beaming.

Grandma Clarrie smiled at Joe. "You're a good brother. But there's more family now to share the loving and the caring. Maybe Francie would like to learn from Taliesin. He's a fine artist, and he doesn't need chatter."

"We saw his workshop. It made her dance with happiness," said Joe.

"And there haven't been any mapmakers in Cruxcia for three generations." Clarrie patted Pa's hand. "It's time there were. Just a suggestion, Leo."

Carrot, who'd been sitting quietly on Joe's arm, regarded the old lady. "She's a good egg."

When it grew dark, Lysander took Joe's rope and wrapped the middle of it around Moustache Man's statue. People ran to grab the ends, including lots of children; someone blew a trumpet fanfare and Lysander called, "Inky, linky, lunky!" They all pulled and the statue popped away from its plinth so easily that everyone toppled onto the ground, laughing.

Vivi called to Lysander, "We should put it somewhere with a notice explaining what he did. As a warning. I'll suggest the Sky Worff as a suitable place at the Council meeting on Monday."

"Hooray!" Hessa hugged her sister. "They've invited you to join."

Lysander thumped Vivi on the back. "Congratulations. High time."

"Only in an advisory role until the elections, of course." Vivi grinned. "Youngest ever. And I'll help decide what to do with Mundle's mansion. All suggestions welcome."

Humphrey had been dozing on Ma's lap, but he sat up suddenly. "I got a sur'gesson, Vivi. When I'm big I'll make you a climbing stairs machine so you can sleep on the roof with us."

Vivi laughed. "Perfect, little cousin," and Humphrey closed his eyes again.

Sal licked an ice cream. She knew she wasn't dreaming, but it was hard to believe this was the same world as a week ago. Every face had come alive with happiness. The trees around the square were lit with lanterns, bright fires burned in braziers, and a half moon had risen above the Societies' Hall. The musicians on the cart were tuning up.

The band played a dance tune and the square filled with

dancers. Tash and Taliesin, Auntie Pi and Nomie, Kestor and Kerala—and Francie. Francie didn't want a partner; she twirled and danced on her own, keeping to the edge of the crowd. Ma held Humphrey on her lap and Sal and Pa watched the dancing together.

"You've done well, Little Bear. So well."

"It turned out all right," said Sal.

"We're together again, and you've found more family."

Sal felt a strange wave of sadness. "You're here. But everything's changed. It won't ever be like it was before."

He stroked her hair. "Nothing stays the same. You're growing up."

Sal hadn't meant to tell him yet but she found herself saying, "I've realised that I don't want to be a mapmaker. I hope you don't mind too much. I just want to study."

"What a good idea," said Pa. "I think that's exactly what you should do." He paused for a moment. "How would you feel if we all stayed here in Cruxcia?"

"And have a house?" Sal's heart soared. "Is that what you and Ma want? I'd like it best of anything."

She looked around. At Ma holding tight to the sleeping Humphrey and laughing with Vivi. At Francie smiling blissfully, dancing a private dance. At Hessa and Joe joining hands and running with a ribbon of children around the dancers. "I think the others like being part of a bigger family as well," said Sal. "Being part of a family who belong somewhere, who make good things happen. Good things for everybody."

"I do, too." He held out his hand. "Shall we join their dance?"

This edition first published in 2021 by Gecko Press
PO Box 9335, Wellington 6141, New Zealand
info@geckopress.com

Reprinted 2022

© Gecko Press Ltd 2021
Text © Eirlys Hunter 2021
Illustrations © Kirsten Slade 2021

All rights reserved. No part of this publication may be reproduced or transmitted
or utilized in any form, or by any means, electronic, mechanical, photocopying
or otherwise without the prior written permission of the publisher.

The author and illustrator assert their moral right to be
identified as the author and illustrator of the work.

Gecko Press acknowledges the generous support of Creative New Zealand.

Gecko Press is committed to sustainable practice in its book publishing.
We publish books to be read over and over and print all new books
on FSC-certified paper from sustainably managed forests.

Edited by Jude Watson
Design and typesetting by Katrina Duncan
Printed in the United Kingdom by CPI Group (UK) Ltd

ISBN paperback: 9781776574049
Ebook available

For more curiously good books, visit geckopress.com